An Invitation

... To the Life of Your Dreams

H. P. Carr

Lavender Press

Published by Lavender Press, London

Copyright © H. P. Carr 2016

www.hpcarr.com

ISBN 978-0-9934879-0-3

The right of H. P. Carr to be identified as the author of this work has been asserted by her in accordance with the Copyright Designs and Patent Act 1988.

All rights reserved. No part of this publication may be reproduced, stored in a retrieval system, or transmitted, in any form or by any means (electronic, mechanical, photocopying, recording or otherwise), without the prior permission of the author.

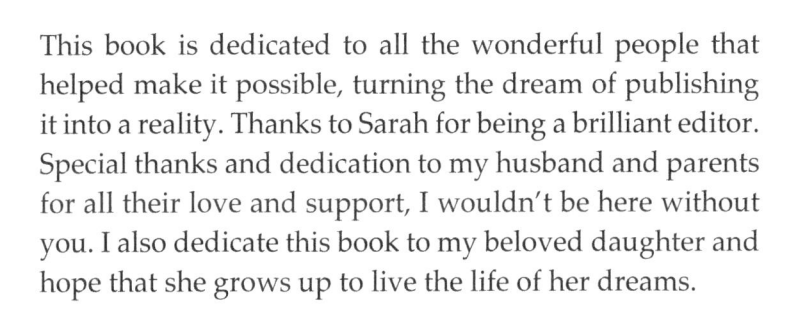

This book is dedicated to all the wonderful people that helped make it possible, turning the dream of publishing it into a reality. Thanks to Sarah for being a brilliant editor. Special thanks and dedication to my husband and parents for all their love and support, I wouldn't be here without you. I also dedicate this book to my beloved daughter and hope that she grows up to live the life of her dreams.

"Imagine if I told you I could transport you
to the life of your dreams.
Are you ready to embark on a journey of deep
discovery to the most amazing places imaginable?"
The voice whispered soft, smooth and
almost inaudible. Did she actually hear it,
or was she just dreaming?

Chapter One

*I would like to invite you on a journey,
to the life of your dreams...*

The invitation gently floated down and settled on the ordinary square straw mat of Jessica Harvey's London town house, early one grey damp Monday morning.

The clatter of the metal letterbox, as the invitation to 'the life of your dreams' burst into her home, woke Jessica from her troubled sleep, sending her obediently to the front door in a trance-like state, to see what bills and junk mail had arrived for her today.

On the mat was a bright bold invitation, the size of a postcard, with words written in beautiful calligraphy, dancing black ink across a bright yellow canvas. She wasn't sure whether it was the appearance of the characters flowing into one another or the impact of the words, but for a brief moment the page seemed to blur and she felt a slight dizziness, which made her close her eyes and take a deep breath. Jessica shook her head and tried to wake herself up as she wondered what the postman was doing coming this early anyway? It was only just starting to get light.

Refocusing on the text, Jessica began to read again. 'I would like to invite you on a journey…'

Stupid junk mail waking me up, I've hardly slept all weekend, she thought as she turned the card over looking for any additional clues. *What hippy nonsense is this? What are they trying to sell me now?*

She felt the rough heaviness of the thick paper in-between her fingers and stared through blurry eyes at the Chinese characters. Beautiful black swirls on yellow, contained within a neat black border. She didn't know what it meant but it looked perfectly balanced, which was far from how she felt.

Jessica shook her head and used the invitation to fan her blurry eyes as she tried to wake herself up, walking back up the stairs almost falling up them. She knew that Pam, her 'professional share' housemate, was never up as early as she was, so it was unlikely she would have to paste on a fake smile and pretend to be sociable, until she got into the office at least.

As she opened the door to her bedroom, out of habit she focused on the dark wooden carriage clock in the centre of the mantelpiece, which had once belonged to her parents. The classic order of the black Roman numerals showed her it was six thirty. She automatically picked up her mobile phone from beside her bed to check the digital display and was horrified to see it read six thirty-four. She lunged for the carriage clock, set it to precisely the correct time, and wound it up as tightly as she could. Jessica needed the clocks to be accurate wherever she went. The deep ticking of time filled the air around her, grounding her and ordering her mind. The man-made rhythm dictated her day, her thoughts, her life.

Tick… Tick… Tick…

Aware of the echo of time cutting through the silence, she tossed the invitation in the bin and scooped up her long, dark-blonde bed hair, twisting it into a neat, orderly bun. She pulled out her trusty black trouser suit, which was actually now far too baggy on her, but came out, like a uniform, when she didn't have the time or energy to think about what to wear, which was often nowadays. She dashed to the bathroom to begin the routine of the day, painting her face with the colour of life she was losing, hiding the lines she was starting to acquire from her thirty-one years.

The constant countdown of the clock seemed to speed up, as did her heart, whilst her mind ran away with her to-do list. She had been thinking about work all weekend, but had been under strict instructions from her boss not to log onto the system, so she was now in a panic about how much awaited her.

Right, I need to get those notes typed up and on the desk by nine, I need to book a room for the nine thirty meeting and arrange invitations for the function, and…

And so it started for another day: a storm cloud of all-consuming thoughts, none of which were her own, raining down and drowning her.

Jessica was the executive assistant for the managing director of a large multinational financial corporation. As such, she was constantly immersed in tactical priorities and corporate strategy. Increasing revenue, improving customer satisfaction and the company's image were all things she went to bed dreaming about. Yet, the funny thing was,

Jessica wasn't even interested in finance or the corporate strategy that surrounded it. In fact, when she let herself admit it, those things bored her deeply.

Ever since the accident ten years ago that turned her life upside down, Jessica had thrown herself into her work. Work consumed her, gave her structure, purpose and a sense of belonging. She didn't need to think about herself, her family, or what she had done. It allowed her to turn her mind into a machine and become almost anonymous to herself and her own life, to forget what had happened.

Whilst Jessica's brain raced through all the hundreds of things she needed to do, and all the things she had to help everyone else do, her body and soul obediently followed, doing as it was told. She was like a robot. Whenever she got tired she would take a shot of caffeine and press on, after all… *time was running out; time was always running out!*

Chapter Two

At eight o'clock Jessica took a deep breath, pasted on a big smile and bounded into the central London office building, full of assertive adrenaline for the tasks ahead. She automatically filed through the lobby security gates and towards the lift, not taking any notice of the fact that the place was unusually empty. The company was at the centre of a financial crisis, and she and her boss had spent weeks looking over options, making cuts across the whole company, including laying off employees. Staff levels had started to go from anxious to absent, and Jessica couldn't lose sight of her role in it all.

I cannot allow my emotions to get in the way, she thought as she desperately tried to turn her mood into a positive one, *the company needs me, Bruce needs me.* Entering the lift, the heavy doors closed in front of her boxing her into the solid metal square. She pressed the button to start the assent to the top floor. *If only we could come up with the solution, instead of spending night after day in the office, staring at the figures and expenditures.* At the thought of her boss Bruce, the lightness she usually felt flutter in her heart was replaced with the heavy emotion she had absorbed from him lately.

She had always admired Bruce, who was usually so smart and handsome, with his neatly groomed black hair, slicked into a side parting disguising the distinguished silver hairs. His expensive well-tailored suits highlighted the physique of a sporty man in his early forties who obviously took care of himself. However, recently he had looked increasingly dishevelled. His hair stuck out all over the place, his un-tucked shirts were creased and messy, revealing he had obviously been working through the night in the office. The boardroom had turned to ruin, hardly recognisable from its former glory. Instead of the normal composure and grandeur the room had commanded over its silent attendees, it had become the critical command centre of 'operation meltdown'. Folders, paper, flipcharts, books, discarded lunch packaging and crumpled scribbled notes overflowing from the table and the bins.

Bruce is really suffering through all of this; I wish I knew what to do. How can I make it better? She thought of how he had previously introduced himself at the many corporate functions and heard his deep booming voice in her head, making her smile: 'Mr Bruce Tailor, Managing Director, at your service' said with a twinkling eye and dazzling smile.

He usually commanded instant respect through his authority and he had a reputation for making girls 'go weak at the knees', but now it was Bruce who seemed weak. Jessica had noticed over the last few weeks that instead of flirting with Anita, the office secretary, and filling the office with his infectious laughter, Bruce had locked himself in the boardroom and not spoken to anyone except Jessica. At first she had been secretly pleased, thinking that she was at the centre of his attention, until she had realised that she was not. His mind seemed far away and distracted, no matter how hard she had tried, she couldn't connect with him.

During the last week, Bruce could be found frantically pacing back and forth in the boardroom, or sitting with his head in his hands, pulling chewed fingernails through his thick greying hair, anxiously stressing out about everything they had to do. The dark stubble, slouched posture, and the look in his eyes, from panic and lack of sleep, made him look menacing.

"What are we going to do?" he would ask Jessica again and again, as if through sleep-deprivation and exhaustion she would magically come up with the answer.

"Do we go with forty per cent staff cuts? Do we sell off part of the business and try and build up what we have left, or negotiate and sell the whole lot? Do we keep selling assets until we have nothing left to sell? Will we have to declare bankruptcy? What are we going to do?" Bruce would repeat in panic.

Jessica still didn't have the answer; she didn't know what they should do. The pleasure she had gained from carrying so much weight within the company and having responsibility and involvement in so many of the decisions, had suddenly come crashing down on her.

I am after all an assistant, not a board member. I'm certainly not paid like a board member and don't get the perks of a board member, she grumbled to herself as the lift started to slow and she reached the twenty-first floor. The lift doors opened. Swallowing hard, she purposely shook her head to dislodge any negative thoughts and forced herself to smile. *I am Bruce's executive assistant and he needs me. The company needs me,* she thought, determined that today would be the day that they would find a solution and make positive change.

She was so motivated to get to Bruce that she whooshed past Anita the office secretary and the empty desks, completely oblivious. Anita got up and was rushing after her, shouting: "Jessica... um... Jess there's something I need to tell you... Jess... JESSICA!"

But it was too late. Jessica threw open the double doors to the wood-panelled boardroom and presented herself with open arms and jazz hands, almost singing "I'm here..." cheerfully and confidently, until the sight before her broke her smile and enthusiasm.

Two men she didn't know, with grey hair and in identical dark charcoal suits, turned to look at her. One was sitting in Bruce's chair and the other perched on the desk; they looked up from the piles of paperwork.

"What... err... who are you?" asked Jessica in shock. She had a bad feeling about these self-important looking men. "Where's Bruce? What's going on?"

"Jessica I tried to tell you but..." pleaded Anita, flustered and out of breath.

"Anita... deal with this, please. I thought we had made it perfectly clear we were not to be interrupted.

Now if you don't mind…" sneered the man perched on the desk, moving his dark gaze back to the paperwork.

"But, where's Bruce…?" demanded Jessica.

The man sitting on Bruce's desk raised his eyebrows and shot Anita a look with piercing eyes. Anita obediently shooed Jessica out of the boardroom and closed the door behind her.

Jessica didn't like the way Anita seemed to have a privileged position in all of this. Secretly she had always felt a little jealous of Anita, stealing Bruce's attention with her giggles and carefree attitude. Now she felt undermined. Anita's luscious long, wavy red hair and immaculate dress sense, with tight pencil skirts and soft silk blouses, showed off her curvy figure perfectly. In comparison, Jessica felt frumpy in her baggy trouser suit and scraped back hair. A strange sense of powerlessness crept through Jessica's body.

"Jessica, I'm sorry but they insisted that they were not to be disturbed. You have to go," Anita said firmly.

"Go? Go where? Where's Bruce?" Jessica tried to be assertive, but her voice came out high-pitched and shrill.

"Bruce has gone," she said shortly, as if this was supposed to make sense.

"Gone where?" Jessica snapped, getting increasingly frustrated.

"He's gone. The board have taken over and they have put everyone on suspended leave until they decide what to do with the company. You should have been sent an email over the weekend telling you not to come in. I'm just here to stop people bombarding them with questions and creating a scene. Which is why you must go."

"But…? What…? Where is Bruce? I should be dealing with this. He would have told me, he would have… Anita?" Jessica pleaded.

"There's a note on your desk. Please Jess, pack up your things and just leave an empty desk. Your pay will continue for the moment and I'll be in touch with everyone once I get more news." Anita's words seemed well practised.

With her hand on Jessica's shoulder, Anita was guiding her to her desk and nodding with staged sympathy.

They can't just get rid of me like that, Jessica thought, feeling a complex mixture of emotions that all cancelled each other out to leave numb confusion. *I'm the managing director's executive assistant for goodness sake. I'm Bruce's confidante, his loyal dedicated Jess, I'm the one person he relies on, I am… I am getting pushed out the door! Pushed out of my company! I don't understand!*

She searched her mind but found nothing that made sense. She tried to call Bruce's mobile but an annoyingly posh lady's voice on an automated telephone system kept telling her that 'the person you are calling is unavailable, please try again later', with no option to leave a message.

She opened the envelope on her desk, which had a very rushed scribble from Bruce using her full name 'Jessica' instead of Jess, which he usually called her.

There was a thick wodge of spa vouchers, which she knew that Bruce had always kept in the safe and given out individually as recognition (and apologies to his wife). She had always longed to get one; each voucher seemed so meaningful and valuable when given in praise. But now, with an envelope full of them, it seemed so trivial. All she had was a solitary sentence scribbled on a compliments slip:

Sorry Jessica, you deserve so much more. Bruce X

Without warning her throat contracted. Tears welled up inside.

NO! she told herself with stubborn anger. *I will not cry, I will not let myself be weak.*

Deep down she knew that if she allowed herself even just a crack of emotion, she would not be able to control it and her whole world would come crashing down around the core of unhappiness she suppressed.

Chapter Three

Since the accident, Jessica had defined herself by her work, giving her a purpose to serve others. She had liked the challenges she had faced as she worked her way up the 'corporate ladder', enjoyed looking after her boss and the business. She used to feel that she was in a very special privileged position as an executive assistant, quietly influencing some of the major decisions. Perhaps naively, she even felt that she could make a real difference to their company and everyone who worked there. Work distracted her from the tragic accident in her past.

Jessica's parents had died in a car accident when she was twenty-one and Jessica blamed herself. The three of them were late to get to her graduation ceremony as she had been trying to decide what to wear. She had spent hours messing about in the mirror with the stupid curls she had put in her hair. Her mother had shouted at her as they left the house to stop being so vain. As they dropped her at the ceremony, so she could get there on time whilst they rushed to find the park and ride, her mother's last words had hurried her along, "Come on Jessica, time's running out." How those words haunted her.

An Invitation . . . To the Life of Your Dreams

How the echoes of ticking time could penetrate her unexpectedly and cause an engulfing wave of sadness to pour into her heart.

Looking around the office for a distraction to fend off the tears, she suddenly caught sight of something tucked into the corner of the noticeboard, jolting her out of the thoughts that threatened to break her. A bright yellow background with a neat black border framed intriguing Chinese characters deep within it. It was the same image she had received this morning, inviting her to the 'life of her dreams'.

Where has that come from? Has someone else received it and put it on the work noticeboard? She picked it up and turned it over. 'Journey to the life of your dreams,' she read with a sense of familiarity and then frustration.

The life of your dreams? How ironic! What life? Huh! she grunted to herself as she put the message in her suit pocket. Somehow she felt compelled to take it, even though she knew it was the public noticeboard and the rules stated that items should not be taken from public display. She was normally always the first to abide by 'the rules'. However, somewhere deep within her it felt like this invitation was a message to her, she was pleased to be able to focus on something outside herself at the moment she most needed it.

As she gathered as many of her belongings into her bag as she could fit, Jessica's thoughts returned to Bruce. *What's happened to him? How can he just leave? Surely he would have told me. He would have said something. I know things are tough but we could have got through it. I'm sure we would have found a way.* Her emotions ran through fear, anger, concern, sadness and overall confusion, all in the space of about thirty seconds. She wasn't sure what to do. How to feel. She was so used to just doing what she was told.

He wouldn't just leave me like this, would he? I thought he needed me. I thought he… She stopped herself, feeling hot tears building up behind her eyes. *No, it's not right, after everything that we've been through and everything I've done for him. He can't just leave me with one scribbled line and an envelope of spa vouchers! I know the financial crisis has been stressful and it's really got to Bruce, but he wouldn't do anything stupid would he?* Her heart started to pound in her chest and she knew she had to do something, anything; action had to be better than this overwhelming sense of uncertainty. She grabbed her car keys, bag and coat and rushed out of the office with even more determination than when she had come in.

I'm going to sort this out. I'll drive to his house and find out what on earth is going on. I'm sure that there is a perfectly logical explanation for all of this. She was down the lift and out of reception in no time. *Yes, that's what Bruce would want me to do. To go to him and sort this all out.*

With increased resolve, Jessica focused on remembering how to drive to Bruce's house. She had often had to take important documents over to his house and had even been over for dinner with Bruce and his wife several times, mainly when she was still with her ex-boyfriend, Steve. However, she found herself driving around roads that all looked the same, desperately trying to recognise something. She put all her thought and concentration into the task at hand, blocking out any emotion or frustration, not allowing herself to think about anything other than finding Bruce.

Eventually, after what seemed like hours of driving up and down numerous residential roads, she came to Bruce's house. By the time she got there it was starting to get dark and she found an empty unlit house with no cars in the drive. No Bruce. No wife. No life.

As no one answered, she wanted to make sure that she had the right house, so she knocked on the neighbour's door to enquire. They said they hadn't seen Bruce for a while. When she asked about his wife, they told her that Bruce had separated from his wife some time ago and that she hadn't been living there for months. Jessica gave them her phone number and they agreed to call if they saw or heard from him.

Why hadn't he told me that he had separated from his wife? she thought, feeling dejected and then anxious. *He's lost his wife, now his job – what next? Oh God, I hope he's ok.*

Chapter Four

Jessica spent the next few days phoning everyone she could think of, friends, business contacts and even his health club, yet despite the anxiety, confusion, concern and restless sleep, Jessica was getting nowhere. She watched the local news religiously and even phoned all the local hospitals but no one seemed to know where Bruce was.

Anita would not tell Jessica anything. She told her 'not to worry', that 'Bruce was fine', even though she refused to give any details. She just kept quoting 'on behalf of the board members…' and saying that everyone was on suspended leave.

Slumped in her chair in the pyjamas she had worn for three days straight, Jessica had no one left to call, nothing else she could think of to do.

Why is this happening? Why am I even stressing out so much over Bruce? Do I need him? Or am I upset because I thought he needed me? Why didn't he tell me about his wife leaving? I thought he would have told me. Would it have changed things between us? Would he have… She didn't allow herself to even think it, as her heart quickened and she suppressed her feelings once more and sat upright in her chair, shaking her head to clear her thoughts.

Her body ached all over, her eyes itched and were streaming with tears of tiredness. Her life, and everything she thought she was and believed in, had disappeared overnight.

An unconscious thought, niggling at her from the back of her mind, wondered if she was just obsessing over her boss to block out the reality of the situation; to give her something to focus on, other than herself. Her work was her life and as such Bruce was everything. She wasn't sure if it was love, admiration or mild obsession, but he was the person she would always put first, above everyone else, including herself. Now it had all been taken away from her, with no explanation. Her mind was swimming with emotions she couldn't control. And she couldn't risk losing control.

As a last attempt to see if there had been any updates in the last ten minutes, she went onto Facebook. She had posted a question asking if anyone knew where Bruce was and had already looked through all of Bruce's friends for clues or photos of him spotted somewhere, but she could find no trace of him.

Maybe Bruce has just gone on holiday, she thought optimistically as she checked his status again for the thousandth time to find nothing. *Maybe he's just decided to give up work and go off to live the life of his dreams.* She smiled.

Over the last few days she had gained a little comfort from seeing life continue as normal through the social scenes and photos on Facebook and Twitter. The world was still out there and life kept on going. It was a strange voyeurism that helped her not feel so lonely; taking her outside her chaotic overcrowded head and placing her in the wider world. She felt like she knew what everyone was up to, without having to actually talk to anyone and explain her situation.

With nothing left to do or check, Jessica needed distraction from her mind. Without realising how or why, she impulsively typed in her ex-boyfriend Steve's name into the Facebook search bar. Her hand stopped mid mouse scroll as she saw Steve had updated new pictures and profile information. From the small thumbnail, the photo looked colourful: yellows and blues, sunshine and beaches. She paused. *Am I really allowed to look at his new life and his photos? The man who loved me, who wanted to marry me?* She wanted to know how he was getting on, but at the same time she didn't want to think about him. She didn't want to think about what had happened and what she had lost. She had spent the last year blocking him out of her memory, keeping herself busy with work, closing down all emotions on the subject.

She walked away from the computer and made herself a sandwich, but her thoughts were consumed with the sunny yellow images and the *should I or shouldn't I* dilemma in her mind.

As she forced herself to eat a dry and dull ham sandwich, she thought back to Steve. On the night he left, he had told her that she was already married to her job and that there wasn't enough space for him in her life. It was true that she always worked long unsociable hours, true that when Bruce called with any request, no matter how trivial, she would drop everything and oblige. Even if it meant that she would never make it to her thirtieth birthday meal, which Steve had specially arranged for her, in one of the most exclusive restaurants in the city. Even if it meant she never saw the corner of the restaurant he had reserved, or the table he had filled with red rose petals and candles, right by the window overlooking the twinkling lights of the city skyline. Even if it meant that she never got to taste the expensive champagne sitting on ice with a crisp white neckerchief tied around it, smart and ready for action, to serve its purpose in the proposal that was to play out.

* * *

Steve had worried that the proposal he had planned may seem cheesy or a cliché, but he also knew that Jessica needed things to be perfect and he had not wanted to disappoint her.

He had arrived early and sat waiting in the restaurant, anxious at first, fumbling in his trouser pocket with the chunky black velvet box and wondering how best to conceal it when she arrived. He had images of her seeing the box before the right moment and making a joke about him being pleased to see her or having a banana in his pocket. As he sat waiting, he started to take the velvet box out of his pocket, to play with it on the table. At first he had been checking it to make sure the ring was still there, an irrational nervousness, which had tricked his mind into the paranoia that it may have somehow disappeared. Like a naughty schoolboy taking a peep at something he shouldn't, checking over his shoulder to make sure he didn't get caught in the act. He had felt like a proud pirate protecting the treasure in its tiny treasure chest, which he was about to share with his woman in a request for her to spend the rest of her life with him.

But the longer he had waited, the longer the box had stayed on the table. Steve had grown more and more frustrated, opening the box and snapping it shut with a violent slap as the lid came down. As time had gone on, he sat there watching other couples come in and then leave again, exchanging curious excited smiles in his direction as they came in and casting pitiful glances as they left. Each passer-by had noticed the empty chair and untouched bottle of champagne, with a white tie around its neck like a noose. They would glance around the room as if looking for the presence of a ghost and then, as he had avoided their gaze and failed to return their pitiful smiles, they had looked at the floor, leaving nothing but whispers as they descended the stairs.

"Oh dear, did you see that?" One couple had said to each other.

"Poor guy… I noticed him on the way in… I think he's been stood up," came the whispers up the stairs.

"I wonder what's happened… how humiliating for him."

It was this final comment that had snapped shut

An Invitation ... To the Life of Your Dreams

the lid on his dreams and his dignity. He opened the box one last time, staring at the solitaire set on a platinum band, the exact size and style Jess liked best, the ring that she was supposed to wear for the rest of her life, but hadn't even bothered to come to collect. The diamond, which had made a huge hole in his bank account, now made a huge hole in his heart, his soul and, if he was to admit it, his pride. He had wanted everything to be perfect; he had tried so hard, as he always did throughout their whole relationship. The only trouble was, as usual, Jessica had not been there.

It had been nearly one o'clock in the morning when Jessica got home, her head numb and exhausted, saturated with financial figures and deal breakers. Despite it being her birthday, Bruce had told her he needed her and so she had stayed to finish the proposal for his deal the next day. She had hardly been able to walk up the three flights of stairs to their small city apartment and all she wanted to do was go to sleep. She had expected to sneak in, go straight to bed next to her boyfriend and then wake up the next day and grovel and apologise for not making the dinner. But there he was, wide awake in the living room, looking at her with cold blue eyes.

"THREE HOURS! I waited three hours in that bloody restaurant, Jessica and you never came," he shouted. She wasn't used to him being so upset with her.

"Huh?" she grimaced, confused as she came in, blinking from the bright lights of their apartment on full.

"Where have you been?" His voice had a flat indifferent tone she wasn't used to.

"Steve, you know where I've been, I sent you a text. I had to get that proposal out. It's a three million pound deal. I'm sorry, but it's only dinner we can do it ano…"

"Only dinner? ONLY DINNER?" he had repeated, his voice had risen in both pitch and volume. He had stood up from the sofa, slapping his hands against his thighs and Jessica had not even noticed the bulge in his pocket. "Only dinner?" he had laughed, as he paced around the room.

"You could have gone ahead without me, just because I'm not there doesn't mean you can't…" she had started quietly, but realised he wasn't up for discussion. She had been too tired for an argument and hadn't realised the significance of that moment.

"That's the trouble Jess, I did go on without you, I went on with plans for the rest of our lives… without you! You are never there!"

Steve had stood still as a statue staring into space, for what had seemed an age. Jessica remembered the overwhelmingly loud silence that had filled the room, sucking the life out of everything as it spilled through the air. She hadn't known what to do, she hadn't realised what was happening, she was too tired and her mind too full of work. The silence of the room had been unbearable and all she could hear was the ticking of her parents' carriage clock of time passing by.

Tick… tick… tick…

"What's it worth?" Steve had eventually said, like

gasping a breath of oxygen, breaking the silence and bringing them both back into the room.

"What do you mean, what's it worth?" she had asked with slight irritation at the depth of the cryptic question. "What's what worth?"

"Your life. Your happiness. Me! What's it worth?" he had asked calmly, not looking at her but instead focusing his non-blinking gaze on a corner of the room. His mind had been made up.

"Steve, I don't unders…"

"You said that the deal for Bruce was three million pounds, so obviously you think that's more important than me, but what about you, your life, your happiness. When are you going to get some perspective? Some balance?"

She had tried to speak, although she had no idea what to say, but he continued. Something in the sadness of his voice and the seriousness of his eyes had made her need to sit down. She remembered it feeling like a heavy weight had pulled her down and frozen her silently to the spot. A cold numbness paralysed her.

"Tonight wasn't just about proposals for a three million pound deal, Jessica. Tonight was supposed to be about a proposal for the rest of your life."

He had pulled out the dark black box and lightly thrown it on her lap. She had felt its heavy thick velvet, knowing what it was without needing to look. She had wanted to say something but no words came out.

"Tonight I waited three hours, an hour for every year that I've waited for you, Jessica. Tonight I wanted to ask you to marry me, but I realise now that you are already married – married to your job!" He had walked over to the sofa, picked up the box and then turned and headed for the door.

"Goodbye, Jessica. I really loved you, you know, but I can't keep going along without you being there. I hope one day you learn to put yourself before your job. You have some serious work-life balance issues and you don't have time for me, you don't even have time for yourself. I can't keep waiting. I'm sorry."

That was it. He was gone and nothing she could do from that moment onwards would ever bring him back. She had lost him forever.

* * *

As she thought back to that evening, Jessica felt a deep sadness in her heart, which she couldn't ignore despite how hard she tried. She had spent all her energy over the last year distracting herself, with work and Bruce, so she wouldn't think about it, so she wouldn't open up to the pain she had so desperately tried to suppress.

Through the power of social and mutual friendship networks, she already knew that Steve had returned the ring, left his job and put all his money towards going travelling around the world. She had seen the odd photo of him wearing a rucksack, sitting with groups of people, playing with kids with wide smiles. However, she had always claimed herself to be too busy to really process what it meant. Too busy to think. Too busy to feel. Too busy to care. That was her excuse anyway, although in reality it was all a pretence. Now, she suddenly had the time, space and opportunity to think and feel, and she felt the danger of the situation. She wished that she could go back in time.

Unable to finish her sandwich, with dry bread sticking tight in her throat, she decided that she should reconnect to Steve on Facebook and stay friends. She told herself that she had every right to look at his status and photos, after all she could have been married to this man by now, plus she wanted to know that he was ok and happy. Her justifications made sense to her as she convinced herself into it.

She went upstairs to her bedroom, sat on the bed and opened her laptop, then clicked on his profile quickly before she changed her mind. His main photo had been updated. There was something uncomfortable stirring within her, there was another person standing next to him. The profile of a woman and the closeness of their bodies, arm in arm and skin on skin, displayed an intimacy she wasn't sure she liked. He was smiling. Really smiling. His profile read, 'Steve is the happiest he's ever been', which instantly sent a stab to her heart. She opened his latest album, her heart beating hard and fast, she felt naughty, like she had no right to be looking at his photos, like she might get caught and someone might actually discover that she cared or had feelings. She pushed those emotions down and looked at the latest photos of him and a gorgeous bronzed blonde goddess. Some photos were with surf boards, holding hands, jumping in the sea, holding each other far too close in wet slippery skimpy swimwear on a sunny beach. She studied his eyes, hoping to see the faint distance she had noticed in their relationship before, but his smiling face lit up the picture, mirrored perfectly by his beautiful female companion.

She felt a sick cold numbness spread over her body like a tsunami engulfing everything around her.

They look so alive, so happy, so full of excitement and adventure. That could have been me. I gave it all up for this… my so called career! Ha, what a joke! Now it's all gone… all of it… forever. She shut the top of the laptop, trying to shut down her senses, sitting lifeless and numb to the pain. The sadness crept up on her up and pulled her into herself, into the burning centre of her emotional lava.

'The happiest he's ever been…' repeated in her mind despite all her efforts to block it. *He must now think back on me and feel pleased that he had a lucky escape. That girl is gorgeous and they look so happy. He must realise now that I was never good enough for him, and laugh at the idea of ever having wanted to be with me.*

She felt sick, worthless, alone and confused. Thoughts and questions scrambled through her mind rapidly. *What had her life become? What was she going to do with her life? What did she even want?*

She lay on her bed with all the questions, emotions and uncertainties swelling like the tide at full moon. She felt a strange sense of presence, a surreal uncertainty, and just at that very moment, in the silence before the surge, she heard the clock.

Tick… tick… tick…

It was the final countdown to the bomb, which was about to go off inside her.

As though watching an old movie in slow motion, it felt surreal, like she was merely in the scene about to unfold. She stood up and picked up her parents' old carriage clock in both hands. She could feel its heaviness, the thick grain and complex inner workings hidden deep inside. She stroked the smooth wood. It was the most precious thing she owned. But it didn't matter anymore. Nothing mattered. Everything was gone.

A strange shouting sound came from the depth of her stomach, she felt like she was exploding from the inside, releasing a raw noise of emotion and suppressed raging pain. She couldn't control it. Couldn't control herself. Every cell in her being felt painfully desperate, stiffening her body and drowning her with despair. All the sadness and grief she had repressed over the years came bubbling up to the surface, radiating out from her heart, causing an explosion of emotions to destroy everything.

Without any sense of reason, she threw the clock against the wall as hard as she could, denting the solid wall and breaking the glass of the clock face into jagged pieces, with bronze metal mechanics springing out of the back. Her body wrenched and convulsed as she threw herself on the bed, heaving sobs causing her back to arch as silent screams seared though her, shaking her body with emotions. She couldn't stop.

Her housemate was at work, but she didn't care if

anyone heard her. Nothing mattered to her anymore. Her body, raw with uncontrollable emotion, gasped for air and she could hardly breathe. She thought she was going to die and she didn't care if she did. She just wanted the emotional pain to stop. It was as if she was possessed. The restless storm waves of unhappiness battered her, shattered and exhausted her, until she was stripped of energy and eventually her body and mind shut down and gave in to sleep.

Chapter Five

She had no idea how many days she had been sleeping on and off in the prison of her room. Her housemate Pam assumed that she was sick and left drinks and chicken soup on the side for her. Jessica pretended to be asleep every time Pam came in, so she didn't have to talk to her. In the middle of the night she managed to get out of bed long enough to eat a bit of the cold soup and finish the drinks.

It was Friday when Pam came home from work and insisted that Jessica got up. Pam was a fiercely strong independent woman, who despite being a very successful and sharp-edged legal assistant at a big law firm had a definite softer maternal side. She was forty-three and had no kids and no serious relationship, and loved it that way. Pam was bright and bubbly, grateful for life, with a loud infectious laugh. Jessica knew that she had left Nigeria with her parents as a young child, but Pam never talked about her past, instead she insisted on 'living in the moment' and always looking on 'the sunny side of life'.

Jessica was groggy and grumpy when Pam came in and it took her a while to focus on what she was saying.

"Hey chickadee, I don't know what's up with you, but you aren't right. Man, this place stinks. You rotting in here? What's going on?" Pam said, opening up the curtains and window and letting the cold fresh air in.

"Please leave me alone," mumbled Jessica, pulling her duvet over her head.

"Hey lady, is that any way to talk to me? I'm just trying to help. I don't know what's up with you, girlio, but you need to stop moping in here and sort it out." Walking towards the door, Pam continued, "You had a call from the dudes at your work."

At that news Jessica sat up straight and blinked at Pam standing in the doorway. "Bruce? What did he say? Where is he?"

"Nah, it wasn't Bruce. That's the boss you obsess over isn't it? Really Jess, you need to sort it out, he's a married man! You said you weren't going to go anywhere near him. It was some posh lady called An-nee-taaaaa." She put on a funny voice to impersonate her.

Jessica groaned and flopped back down to her bed, pulling the duvet up to her chin. Pam, sensing Jessica's deflated reaction, came and sat down on the bed beside her, taking a softer tone.

"She told me what's happened, that you are all on leave whilst they work out packages. She said it would be some time before a decision is made and that you should continue on suspended leave until further notice, but you will be paid. Is that what this is all about, Jess? Is that why you are in this state? Come on, it's only a job! Man, I wish I was being paid to do nothing!"

An Invitation ... To the Life of Your Dreams

Jessica turned to face Pam, with snotty bed hair stuck to her face.

"Good God, woman. Have you had a look at yourself?" Pam said, grabbing a mirror from the side and thrusting it at her. "I'm going to go and run you a bath."

"No, I…" Jessica started, but was cut short.

"Err… no, lady, you're having a bath – you're a public health risk decomposing up here. I'm having some friends over tonight and I don't want them thinking I keep a person locked up here. You're having a bath and then joining us for a very, very large glass of wine or three downstairs. I'm not taking no for an answer." Pam strutted off to the bathroom and Jessica heard the taps turn and water gush out. She knew there was no point fighting it and that she had no choice but to do as she was told.

Jessica sat up and looked in the mirror, not recognising who she saw. She observed the strange person's face as though looking at an animal in the zoo. Her eyes were all puffed up, her face red and raw with emotion; her hair was all over the place, strands stuck to her face. Jessica was bemused by the person she saw in the mirror, like recognising someone who cannot be placed. She certainly looked very different from the tightly wound professional business women she usually presented to the world. Pam appeared a few minutes later and gently coaxed her to the bathroom. Jessica creaked and groaned as she got up and moved, aching all over and feeling as if she were one hundred and thirty-one years old.

Pam had run a hot bath with bubbles and candles

and poured her a glass of wine, telling her that she would see her afterwards. Jessica took a sip of the warming red wine and looked at the effort her housemate had put into setting the scene. *I can't be completely ungrateful and selfish,* she thought, as she obediently stripped off and immersed herself in the tub.

Soaking in the hot steaming water she started to get her senses back. She could smell the sweet scented soap and feel the water against her skin, washing away the salty residue of tears. She created gentle waves, which turned into ripples, resonating all around her, then disappearing to leave it still and calm again. She realised that, although she felt drained and still a little numb, she needed to make the decision to take back her life.

***

That night, Pam invited Jessica to join her friends Suzie and Emma as they all stayed in and consumed several bottles of wine with a takeaway. Gradually, Jessica found herself smiling and then even laughing as they shared funny stories with intimate details, about their lives, work, colleagues, lovers, bosses and friends.

"Right Jess, you moody moo, I've got a game for you," Pam jested, gathering everyone together by clinking her wine glass with her oversized colourfully jewelled ring. "Everyone listen up, we are going to play the get-it-out-your-system game. Jess here is feeling a little down, she's lost her job and her boss, who she seemed to love way too much if you ask me. The girl's got issues. But heck, don't we all? Let's play 'I've got issues…'" She cheered and Suzie and Emma joined in, keen to get involved. "Who wants to start?" Pam threw it open. Suzie and Emma were obviously used to this familiar de-stressing tactic of Pam's and joined in straight away.

"Oooh, I'll go first," said Suzie, a bubbly brunette who worked in corporate sales. She sat up straight, facing Jessica and proudly announced, "I've got issues… right? I have been single for… like… ever. I don't understand. Where are all the nice and normal men? All I seem to attract are weirdos."

"Oooh, I like the weirdos," laughed Pam, winking at Jessica.

"Seriously, where is my Mr Right?"

"Who would be your Mr Right?" Jessica asked politely. "What's your type?"

"Oh I don't know. Normal. Nice. Breathing!" Suzie laughed.

"You've got to know what you're looking for in order to find it, otherwise how will you know when you have found him," Emma said earnestly.

"So did you know what your man looked like before you met him?" Suzie responded to Emma.

"No, not what he looked like, not really, but the qualities I was looking for, that he would need to have. I dreamed about what he would be like and then when I met George I just knew he was the one."

"So you are the lucky one Emma, you've got your Mr Nice and Normal, tell me the secret?" Suzie nudged her.

"Ha, there is no secret. In fact… If we are playing the game, then I've got issues too… I've been with George for ten years now and he's still not proposed, I'm not sure if he ever will. I'm thirty-five already and want to have children, but all he seems interested in is going out and getting drunk with his mates. Not sure whether to stick it out, or leave him and try and find someone else before it's too late."

"Well, I just wanna be single," Pam said assertively. "I can do what I want, when I want and I don't have to answer to anyone or feel second best to… football or whatever. And besides… I am just too hot to handle," she said standing up and strutting her stuff as the other girls all erupted into laughter. "Go on then Jess, your turn," said Pam.

"Well, I am not sure that I want to talk about my issues. I am also single, I lost my 'Mr Nice and Normal' who did want to marry me, but I was working way too much and I put my boss first. But now I've lost my job and my boss has disappeared, so it's all a bit screwed really," Jessica said out loud, but instead of feeling sad she was actually laughing at how ridiculous it all sounded.

"I wish my boss would disappear," said Suzie after hearing about Bruce. "She's a witch!"

"Ha, the wicked witch of the western working world," laughed Pam. "What's she done this time?"

"She wouldn't hire this really amazing lady last week because she wasn't wearing tights! I mean, come on?" Suzie exclaimed.

"She wasn't wearing tights?" Emma scoffed.

"Really?"

"Yep!" Suzie continued. "She said that she obviously didn't know 'the rules of business' if she didn't even know how to dress appropriately."

"She's got a bit of a thing about dress hasn't she, your boss, I remember you mentioning it before?" said Pam.

"Yeah," Suzie said, turning to Jessica to explain. "She's like a throwback from the eighties, all short hair and shoulder pads, she thinks that women should be men: act like men, dress like men. She is very harsh on other women. Heaven forbid you had a bit of a bare shoulder showing or were dressed femininely with high heels and a skirt above the knee. You'd think we were living in Victorian times. Honestly. I know it's the corporate world, and I like that she is tough and tells it like it is, but sometimes it's just exhausting having to be the perfect image they want you to be."

"It just goes to show," said Emma, "you never know how people may take offence over work wear. I always tend to dress in safe, conservative suits, even though it's boring. Although it does tend to look like we're going to a funeral sometimes. My wardrobe is full of black, grey and blue; I don't even have any nice clothes for the weekend. It's so sad." Emma did a fake sob into her wine.

"WHAT?" exclaimed Pam topping up everyone's wine. 'I've gotta take you girls shopping, life is for the weekend, you've gotta own it! Surely you've got a pulling party dress? Everyone needs one of those."

"I don't have a pulling party dress," cried Suzie,

concluding, "maybe that's why I don't pull," and they all laughed.

"Ok, let's fix a date to go out on the prrrrowwll," Pam purred and clinked glasses with Suzie. "Right ladies, come and have a look at my dresses and see if there's any you'd like to borrow. We need a makeover and a move-over-here-we-come night!"

With that they grabbed another bottle of wine and went up to Pam's room. Jessica stayed downstairs at first but was drawn up by the sound of infectious laughter, diving into the carnage of clothes being flung everywhere as the girls modelled some of Pam's dresses.

For the first time, in what felt like a long time, Jessica realised that she was all right. She was relaxed. She had released all the tension and emotion, which had been stored up inside her. Whilst she felt a little weak and uncertain about the world she had just woken up in, she felt a quiet stillness within herself and the world around her.

"You know, you're all right, our kid," said Pam, on her third bottle of wine. "I used to think you were a right stuck up prude, but you're actually human. I like that. You're all right with me," she slurred, as she drunkenly hugged her friend and they both collapsed in a heap of giggles on the pile of clothes on the bed.

Chapter Six

The morning after the night before was a bit of a blur. Jessica felt hazy as she tried to make sense of what had happened last night as well as the entire last week. In fact, she was waking up from the lifeless existence of her last few years.

At first she didn't know what to do with herself, it was as if she had fallen down a black hole. She wasn't used to having time to herself. Suddenly she had no structure or rules by which to live; she no longer could define herself by her work. She used to think about work every day, every night and even weekends, never letting go. However, she had absolutely no driving urge to go out and find another job. Her body and mind felt exhausted and she knew she had to take some time out for herself.

She tucked herself up under a blanket, watching TV from the sofa like a sick person, just without any of the sneezing and sore throats. She felt a guilty pleasure, as she did nothing, knowing that her housemate and everyone else were at work. She allowed her mind to fill with the nonsense on TV, which was comforting at first. She watched cookery demonstrations as if she were actually interested, listened to advice on sexual health problems, and watched soaps she had no idea about. At last she could take no more when a talk show's guests had a fight, over a drug induced affair, and the aggressive shouting all got too much for her and she turned it off.

Well, it could be worse, she thought cheerfully as she packed up the blanket, with a little hope and perspective, realising that she wasn't a total mess. Needing to do something, she decided to go on-line.

She was so used to having her laptop glued to her at all times that it felt quite strange not having it on and whirring beside her, consuming her life with emails and trivial things from her never ending 'to-do' list. She remembered the spa vouchers she had been given, which said that they were redeemable at most spa resorts across the country. She did an internet search and was overwhelmed by the choice. There were so many options, her head started to spin again and she had no idea where to start.

I thought the whole point of a spa is that it is supposed to be relaxing, she sneered to herself. *So why am I finding it so stressful? Health spas, beauty spas, dietary spas, yoga spas, aqua spas… I have absolutely no idea what I should be doing.*

She decided to go and make herself a cup of tea, there was too much information and yet none of it seemed to be appealing to her. As she waited for the kettle to boil, she picked up the local paper and the usual advertisements for double glazing and carpet cleaning companies fell out. She scooped them up

An Invitation ... To the Life of Your Dreams

and, as she threw them into the bin, a yellow leaflet fell and landed next to her foot. There were those Chinese characters again, bold black on sunny yellow, like a bumblebee pollinating her thoughts.

Picking it up, the Chinese characters intrigued her. A horizontal box split by a straight line perfectly down the middle, dividing the rectangle into balanced halves. The character next to it looked like a stick man trapped inside a box, but with one side released so he could get out if he just turned his head and saw the opportunity. She would later find out that these were the traditional characters for Chinese Medicine.

Man, their marketing is good, they must be really looking for business, she thought, opening the leaflet. It was a holistic health and wellbeing centre, which offered a whole range of treatments from conventional massage to yoga and meditation. It said that the centre used Traditional Chinese Medicine, offering a medical massage called Tui Na and acupuncture. She was scared of needles so didn't want to try acupuncture, but she was interested in the Chinese medical massage, especially as it said it was done on top of light cotton clothing. She wouldn't have to lie naked on a slab whilst a stranger rubbed and prodded her, which is a fear she always had with massage.

"Well in that case," she announced proudly to the empty room. "I had better try it out. I think I've found my spa!"

She called the number and asked if they accepted the national spa treatment vouchers, which Bruce had given her. The man on the phone wasn't sure and she could hear him talking to someone in the background. She started to tell them her name and phone number, but as she did the phone was suddenly passed to a Chinese woman who interrupted her mid-sentence.

"Jessica, yes? Jessica Harvey. Yes. You come – when? Tomorrow?" The thick Chinese accent and friendly nature of this woman made Jessica smile.

"Errr, tomorrow…? Yeah sure, I can do that."

"Yes? Good, good, Jessica. Ten thirty?" said the lady, radiating such a warm familiarity that Jessica felt like a long-lost friend was greeting her.

"Ten thirty is fine," she confirmed. "I look forward to finding out more about your place, I've seen so many of your leaflets, they seem to be everywhere."

"When the student is ready the teacher appears," the Chinese lady concluded.

Chapter Seven

Intrigued as to what she might encounter at the 'holistic and wellbeing centre', Jessica did some investigating on the computer that night. The website said that Tui Na had been used for more than four thousand years by Chinese and athletes for peak performance and health. It claimed to balance and harmonise the body, build up the immune system and could treat problems associated with the modern lifestyle, including stress and injury.

Jessica felt pleased that she was about to begin something that might actually bring some balance to her life after all, she had heard so many times that she needed to get work/life balance but never really knew how.

She linked through to other websites and read all about Qi (pronounced 'chee'), learning that the Chinese translate this as 'breaths' and believe it to be 'the vital force of life' or 'activating energy, flowing through the universe'.

She also read a famous quote by Wang Chong (AD 27–97), which fascinated her:

> Qi produces the human body
> just as water becomes ice.
> As water freezes into ice,
> so Qi coagulates to form the human body.
> When ice melts, it becomes water.
> When a person dies, he or she becomes spirit again.
> It is called spirit, just as melted ice changes its name to water.

The websites went on to say that when Qi is balanced, your body is 'strong and healthy, free from aches, pains and illness and you feel completely confident and relaxed'.

"Sounds blooming marvellous," Jessica said out loud, intrigued to find out if it would really work for her, or if it was just going to be another funny experience she could laugh with Pam about over a glass of wine.

* * *

The next morning, Jessica bounded to the holistic health centre, her stomach tightly coiled with anticipation of the unknown.

Suddenly unused to the lack of routine and structure, Jessica had overslept and was running late, something she never used to do.

Rushing into the centre, panting and out of breath, everything suddenly seemed to stop. The space inside the centre was very white and light, airy and still. The silence struck her. It made her ears ring with the echo of noise that had suddenly just stopped. The centre was like an old photograph she had once seen of a person standing still in the middle of a busy blurred scene; people hurrying past, no one noticing the stillness right there in the middle of it all.

"Hello, Jessica," said an older plump Chinese woman, with white hair pinned back.

How does she know who I am? Have I met this lady before? Jessica wondered, feeling like she somehow knew her on a deeper level. *I don't think that I've met her before, but she seems so certain to know me.* The thought flashed through her mind with a strange sense of uncertain familiarity, before Jessica returned to the present moment with a shake of her head.

Jessica smiled and tried to compose herself, not wishing to draw attention to her lack of experience at these things. She felt less sure of who she was than this stranger seemed to, whose certainty and familiarity was somehow comforting.

"I will get Dr Wu," said the lady softly, with a knowing smile and shining eyes. She turned through a circular door out into a sunny courtyard.

What am I getting myself into here? thought Jessica, trying to analyse the lady's almost mischievous smile and expectant eyes.

Before Jessica had time to further speculate on the woman's familiar response, a tall handsome Chinese man with thick dark black hair came through, dressed in a long white shirt and loose linen trousers.

"Thanks, Aunty." Jessica heard him say to the woman who did not re-emerge.

Jessica's first impression was that he seemed too young to be a doctor, although maybe it was just his youthful skin, which was flawless. She estimated that he must be mid-thirties, but he held a child-like innocence about him through his bright shining eyes.

"Please go through and sit down," he said gently, indicating through to a room off the side of reception, opening up his hand to direct her, allowing her to walk in first. Something about his commanding calmness gave him an authority that made her giddy.

She walked through a doorway and hesitated, wondering where she was supposed to sit. There was a massage table, like a single bed, with large soft cushions. Next to it were two white chairs beside a low table, made from bamboo, with a beautiful purple orchid in the centre. There were endless shelves of books, with posters and charts pinned to the wall depicting the human body and blurs of colour and patterns within it. Hundreds of tiny bottles of aromatherapy oils stood proud on the shelves of a tall cabinet, like teeny terracotta warriors. Underneath the bottles were lots of little drawers, which could have been full of anything. A couple were open and looked like they had bags of leaves in them. Like a child in a sweet shop, she wanted to open all the drawers, to discover all the tiny treasures hidden inside, to explore and take it all in.

Without speaking, the young man gently glided towards her, guiding her to the two chairs with subtle gestures and she sat down obediently. She tried to make nervous conversation by expressing her enthusiasm for the surroundings and the smell of essential oils as she entered, but he did not engage. They sat for the first couple of moments in silence, he didn't say anything, he simply sat looking at her. His eyes were a warm brown, his face was kind and his golden skin glowed, radiating life and positive energy.

Feeling very aware and conscious of herself and her surroundings, she had no idea what to say.

Should I just stare back at him, she wondered. *Is this like the staring competitions we used to have at school? Is he looking into my soul? Is that what they do? I wish he would just get on with it.*

She broke the stare and unsure of where to look read a framed quote which hung on the wall, written in beautiful black calligraphy:

> All that we are
> is the result of what we have thought.
> The mind is everything.
> What we think we become.
> – Gautama Buddha

"So…?" she said at last, looking at him again, awkwardly shifting in her seat and making big exaggerated circular hand gestures. She at least expected him to respond, but he continued to sit silently and smile at her.

Finally, he took a breath and with a twinkle in his eye slowly replied, "So…? Where's the tiger?"

Relieved for a split moment that he had eventually spoken and broken the silence, which held dangers for the chattering of her nervous mind, she relaxed slightly and adjusted her position in her seat. Then, absorbing the meaning of the words he had just said, she felt confused again. She looked at him bewildered.

"You have a lot of adrenaline running through you," he said with a soft kind voice. "This is a human response for when you need it, when there is a tiger, when you need to run or fight an attack. It is not good to run on adrenaline all the time, it is not natural to the body."

She continued to look at him, expressionless. She suddenly noticed the difference between their energy levels and she felt noisy, shuffling in her chair trying to get comfortable.

"Modern society and stressful jobs often push us to run on adrenaline, but it's not good to keep pushing your body, making it prepare to fight tigers, then just sit still in an office and do nothing physical. When sitting still, the body should be relaxed, when fighting tigers, the body should be ready with adrenaline."

She nodded obediently, half drawn to his kind eyes and half bemused by what he was saying.

Wait until I tell Pam and the girls about this one tonight, she smiled to herself.

"Now, put your hands on the lower part of your stomach, so that your fingers are just touching," he said, as he demonstrated interlocking his own long slender fingers across his tummy. Like a proud pregnant lady holding her baby bump, she felt a slight roll under her fingers and felt embarrassed that she was getting out of shape.

"Do not worry about the leftovers from Christmas," he said kindly, grabbing an almost non-existent roll of his own smooth skin and smiling. She burst out laughing and instantly felt better.

"Now, take a very deep breath in through your nose, opening up your diaphragm so that your belly pushes out, like a balloon filling up with air, and your fingers are no longer touching. Hold for as long as you can and then gently and slowly release, in a controlled way through your mouth, until all the air has emptied. If you want, you can count to four as you inhale, hold, then exhale for a count of eight."

They sat there breathing deeply for a few minutes, until she no longer felt stupid, she no longer felt anxious, she no longer felt self-aware. She started feeling relaxed. Every breath she took, cleansed her and filled her with the oxygen her body needed. Her mind was full only of the process of breathing.

"The body relaxes when it breathes properly and the oxygen replenishes us and helps us think, act and control our responses," Dr Wu explained.

"That sounds good," Jessica half laughed, but Dr Wu didn't smile, he just looked calmly into her eyes with a penetrating warmth. He seemed to unlock something in her and she surprised herself by the calm safety she felt.

"To be able to control our responses..." she clarified, still his face was a blank canvas, as if waiting in anticipation. She felt like he was inviting her somehow to open up, inviting her to provoke a response from him. Unable to accept the silence, she continued, "I seem to have had difficulty recently controlling my emotions. I can't seem to hold myself together. I feel like crying all the time. I want to shut out the world and to wake up when it's all over. I just want it to be over." She paused as a lump caught in her throat and she couldn't speak anymore.

"What do you want to be over?" Dr Wu calmly coaxed.

"Everything! Just… well, everything's gone wrong in my life, it's all fallen apart. I've fallen apart and I don't know how to pull myself back together." He sat silently with a gentle expression, inviting her to continue to talk.

"I just lost my job and, well, I kind of defined myself by my work. I know that might sound stupid but… it was the only thing I had left. I pushed away all my friends, lost the only boy who ever loved and put up with me, and… my p-p-parents," she stuttered, but could not continue as tears rolled out of her eyes and down her cheeks. Dr Wu put a firm hand on her shoulder and handed her a box of soft white tissues. She wiped away the tears and found the strength to continue.

"They died ten years ago, it was my fault. I was late and being vain and they rushed to park for my graduation ceremony and crashed into a lorry and their car overturned and fell from a bridge." It all came tumbling out of Jessica as she hardly paused for breath. "They said it was instant, that they wouldn't have felt any pain, but the last words we ever said to each other were in frustration. I wish I could take it all back, to have left on time. I was so selfish that during the ceremony, before I knew what had happened, I was actually annoyed at them for missing my graduation. Their last moments alive were filled with my frustration. I wish I had been a better daughter, I wish I was a better person. I was so caught up in myself, in my stupid trivial nonsense. I haven't, I cannot, forgive myself." She poured her heart out to this stranger as he sat and listened, reassuring her to continue with subtle nods and understanding sympathetic smiles.

"It is important to release this energy," he said at last when she could no longer speak through her tears. "Everything is energy: our thoughts, our bodies, this table." He knocked on the bamboo wood as he continued. "The chair you are sitting on, the tears you are crying. Some energy we can see, it has materialised and we can touch and feel and understand it. Other energy is invisible to the eye, but we can feel it. We hold it deep inside. The thing with energy is that we cannot and should not hold onto it. Like a meandering river, it needs to move, to flow, to exist beyond our control. If we try to hold onto energy for too long it will eventually break us down, like a dam made of twigs, to pass on its journey. We must let it go."

He gently took her shoulders in his hands and straightened her up, mirroring her with his own posture. He bowed his head down close to hers, to catch her eye and then lifted his head back up, encouraging her to do the same and look up from her lap, where her gaze had been fixed. Her hands fiddled, as though weaving imaginary string through and round her fingers, knotting it tighter and tighter. He took her hands in his and gently placed them on her lap. He softly touched the underneath of her chin with his finger to bring her face up into view. Her eyes were so full of tears, she could hardly see.

"Every moment, every aspect of your life, good and bad, has been leading you here and now. That is all we can ever have, the present moment. We cannot control the past or the future, we can only live in the now. Similarly, we cannot control every situation, only our response to the situation itself. You have been through a lot, and it is good to cry and release the energy. You must not try to hold onto it. It will not bring your parents back, or your work, or your boyfriend. You must focus your energy on what you can influence, on what you want, so that you can make the life you have been given, this wonderful gift of life, as exceptional as possible."

He stood up and gently started moving Jessica's body, like an artist carefully positioning his subject ready to craft. "You can control your posture, which can change the energy of how you feel. Just trust me a moment…" he said, as he pulled her up in her chair from her slouched position, gently straightened her spine from the base all the way up to her head with his hand, which felt warm and soothing to Jessica. She was now sitting up straight with both feet firmly flat on the ground, her hands on her lap, head held up and shoulders down. Jessica felt a shift in her energy. She noticed that she had stopped crying. Dr Wu asked her to close her eyes and focus on her breathing, clearing her mind of all thoughts and emotions.

"If thoughts creep into your mind, that's ok," he reassured her, "they will. But remember you can control your response to them. You can observe your thoughts and politely ask them to keep flowing on through you, they are, after all, just energy. Like clouds passing by, there will be storm clouds and light fluffy clouds, don't worry about what type of clouds they are, just let them flow by. And remember, it takes sunshine and rain to make life grow."

After several deep breaths in and out, clearing her flow of energy, Dr Wu started to tell her the story of the sequoia tree, in a deep calm voice.

"When you think of trees and fire, you think that the fire would destroy a tree, right? That the tree couldn't survive if it were burnt by a raging forest fire. However, some of the longest living and largest trees in the world actually need fire to grow, to reproduce. It's a process of renewal. The fire opens up new opportunity for the sequoia tree to grow, clearing overpopulated areas, to let in sunshine, whilst the ash enriches the soil with fertile nutrients. The tree's cones actually need the heat from the fire to open and release their seed. Without it, they would not flourish. Like the circle of life. We are all born and we all pass, yet the life all around us continues. The universe is abundant and we can tap into that flow of energy and use it to create transformation and growth, providing we allow it to flow and do not try to hold onto something that we cannot control. Allow yourself to be in the moment, not stuck in the past or concerned with the future. Hear your breath and the sounds in the room. Feel your body on the chair you are sitting on, the firmness and constant support of the earth beneath you, supporting you no matter what."

Dr Wu guided her back into the room, reconnecting her with her surroundings. As she opened her eyes, she was pleased to see him smiling through his deep brown eyes, as she brought her attention back into the room and into the moment.

"There is a lot to release and a lot to rediscover. There is no rush. There are no tigers here," he said with smiling eyes that seemed to soothe her to the soul.

"Come..." he said standing up and lightly cradling her elbow, raising her from her seat and guiding her out of the room, their arms interlinked. He led her through the circular doorway, into a calm oasis of a walled courtyard garden. The air smelt clean and crisp, it felt fresh against her hot and tear-stained rosy cheeks.

"Sit here a moment, I will get us some tea," he said, as he released her arm.

"How does no one know that this place exists in the middle of the city?" she said as he turned to walk back through the circular doorway. "It's magical."

"There are always places of tranquillity and calm, you just have to find them." He gave her a smile before slipping back inside, leaving her alone in the moment.

In the centre of the courtyard was a bubbling water fountain, cascading water onto rocks and into a round pool. Water lilies stretched out, balanced perfectly on the shimmering water, and she could see colourful carp meandering between the leaves. Trees with beautiful pink and white blossom curved above her, casting shadows as the branches slightly swayed in the breeze. A whole orchestra of songbirds chirped and she could feel the sunshine on her face. Beyond the fountain was an arch of green, leading through to more trees and foliage. She longed to explore, yet she felt content and peaceful in the present moment. She sat on a large smooth rock dipping her fingers lightly into the water, creating gentle ripples, which attracted the attention of the fish.

"The fish are lucky. And they like you," said Dr Wu, smiling as he returned, handing Jessica a cup of steaming sweet jasmine tea.

"They just think I'm dinner," replied Jessica dismissively, as the ripples she had made with her finger faded away and the fish dispersed.

"Many are affected by the ripples we create, but because we are usually at the centre, it is not always possible for us to see."

They sat in serene silence, listening to the birds and savouring the hot steaming tea. Once they had finished, Dr Wu stood up and beckoned her back inside.

"You need to quieten your mind from the constant chatter and reconnect with your inner resource, your deeper consciousness and the strength of your being," he said calmly as he guided her back through into the treatment room, which looked more familiar and comfortable to Jessica now as they sat back down.

* * *

"What would you do if you knew you couldn't fail? If you didn't need to work for money, what would you do with your time and why?"

"If I were rich you mean? Like if I won the lottery?" she shot him a twinkling smile at the idea.

"Well, that depends on how you personally define the term rich," he said, mirroring her smile. "It is deeply subjective and absolutely relative. Some who have very little money or possessions can feel richer than those living in palaces. Some may say that to have good health and access to basic needs like food, water and shelter is winning the lottery of life. It is our gratitude and appreciation for what we have that makes us feel rich."

"Oh, well, I err… I have no idea," she slurred, her smile fading as she tried to think seriously but was genuinely at a loss.

"The reason I ask you this, is that so many of us define ourselves by our job, how much we earn, or what possessions we have. We feel that we have to conform to someone else's ideals in order to survive, passively following the latest fashions and advertising campaigns in order to be seen as successful. It is easy to sleep walk through life without ever questioning why: why are we here, why do we do what we do, and what's the bigger purpose outside ourselves?" He paused to allow Jessica time to think through these big life questions, before continuing, "There is often something tapping away at our soul, our consciousness. Something that niggles away at us but which we try to ignore, until it gets louder and louder, and even then, we often make excuses as to why we cannot listen." He looked deeply into her eyes and she felt a need to have an answer, although she had no idea what to say.

"I think I'll need to give it some time to think it over," she blurted out, trying to buy some time, whilst he continued to look at her expectantly. "I guess that I have to find myself, my own passions and dreams. I don't want to exhaust myself with meaningless tasks, spending all my time working for someone else anymore, I want to find some time for myself."

"That's good, Jessica," he gently reassured her, and she let out a deep sigh of relief.

How can I not know what I want out of life? How had I never asked myself this before? Jessica thought with sudden awareness.

"You attract and create what you think about, therefore, you must always focus on what you want, not on what you don't want. Your subconscious doesn't differentiate between a positive and a negative statement. The classic example being, 'do not think about pink elephants'. Even though it's a negative command, you can't help but think about pink elephants as it plants this thought into your mind. Therefore, you must turn any negative thought into a positive, always focus on what you want. So instead of saying I don't want to spend all my time working for someone else, you could say, I would like more freedom of my time. I would like to work for myself, or to do what I enjoy, work that is meaningful to me. Does that make sense?"

"Err… I think so," she said slowly, trying to follow his logic.

"People are often driven by fear rather than genuine passion of purpose. Fear of failure and even fear of success paralyses us, keeps us happily plodding along in our daily routines and our comfort zones afraid to try anything else. The voice of doubt in our minds, the negative statements, block us and stop us doing what we love. Therefore if you hear yourself thinking negatively, try and turn the statement around into a positive. It will take time to make this way of thinking a habit. Masters of greater spiritual and intellectual powers dedicate their lives to it. But it's worth taking the time to train and exercise our brain as our mind is the most powerful thing we own; our thoughts create our reality. How often do you take time to sit with yourself, to quiet your mind and the noise of your busy life to ask yourself what do you really want from life? What is meaningful to you? What is your purpose?"

"But I don't have time for all that," she brushed him off, feeling frustrated and defensive, fidgeting on her chair.

"It is true… if you believe it to be so. If you don't believe that you have time, then you won't have time. Time cannot be controlled, only your perception of it can. You can choose how to spend your time, to decide what is most important to you and what to focus your mind on. You are in control of your own destiny, no one else. Everyone has the opportunity to create time for something that's important to them, otherwise you are allowing others to dictate your day, your time, your life. You are sleepwalking through someone else's dream."

"Ok," she sulked. "But what do I do once I've made some time? Just sit there in silence waiting for my soul to talk to me?" she said sarcastically, suddenly not enjoying being challenged. He didn't understand how busy her life had been, how she didn't even have time to go to the loo let alone take time out to meditate or whatever he was suggesting.

"You can calm your mind by focusing on your breathing, deep breaths in and out, like we did earlier. Search deep within yourself by asking yourself the questions and listening to how you feel to gain the answers. If you need to make decisions, feel the response of your energy as you go through each option. What gives you the most energy, makes you feel really excited, inspired, passionate, alive? Follow these feelings, they are your intuition, the signposts along your path to happiness, fulfilment and achieving complete richness in life. Your intuition is your map and compass to the hidden treasures within."

Dr Wu wanted to allow her mind to relax and absorb all that he had said, whilst he worked on the physical.

"Now, I am going to give you an initial Tui Na massage to loosen the muscles, to try and release some of the tension. It will help realign your energy and chakras. Then we can start a course of balancing treatments," he said, standing up and gesturing for her to do the same. "Do you have any back pains at all?" he asked.

"Yeah, actually I get pains in my back sometimes," she said, rubbing her hand on the base of her spine. "I think it might be from sitting at a computer all day," she continued.

"It could be," he said placing his hand over her lower back, which surprised her by instantly feeling warm. "We weren't designed to sit still hunched over a computer all day, especially if we feel stress and do not move to release the tension. The lower back pain could also be a block in your muladhara."

"My mula-what-a?" she laughed.

"Your muladhara is your first chakra, the base chakra. It sits around your first three vertebrae and pelvic floor, it relates to your sense of security and what grounds you in life. Blockages in this chakra may result in back pain, constipation, colon or bladder problems and even fear and anxiety disorders. It's a good place to start as balancing this chakra will help you feel secure and at peace, as well as creating a solid foundation for working on the other chakras."

"Err... What are shack-rars?" Jessica enquired sheepishly, not sure if she was pronouncing it correctly, or asking a really dumb question, having never heard of any of this before.

"Chakras are like swirling masses of energy that correspond to nerve and organ centres in our body and allow vital energy to flow through us. We have seven main chakras from the base of our spine to the crown of our head and they need to be open and in alignment to keep us healthy and full of vitality." She was trying to listen and absorb what he was saying, whilst climbing onto the massage bench.

"Physical ailments and emotional distress can

often be linked to blockages in our chakras, so it's important to keep these in balance," he continued.

"Oh," was all she could muster in response, as she positioned herself carefully face down, not really understanding what he was saying.

"It's like a blocked sink. Have you ever come across a blocked sink that starts to smell and the water doesn't drain properly?"

Jessica thought back to university and the kitchen sink in their busy student house that was always full of dirty dishes, with slimy vegetables and old baked beans in the plughole. The water would take forever to drain and the drainage system stank. "Yes," she confirmed, curling up her nose as she remembered the stench.

"If it's blocked, the water cannot flow through properly. It stagnates, bacteria grows and the blockage gets worse as it attracts more waste and clogs up further. Well similarly, if our chakras get blocked, the energy cannot flow through freely. Keeping our chakras open and in flow is vital for our health, balancing the whole mind-body energy system."

Jessica was happy to take his word for it and hope he knew a lot more than she did about how to unblock her chakras. She chuckled to herself as she thought that she certainly didn't want to be like the smelly old sink at university.

She lay on the bed fully clothed with her head resting on a lavender scented pillow. At first, she felt very aware of herself and the male presence beside her, who was about to touch her body. Thoughts rushed through her head making her heart quicken. *Am I lying correctly? How long will this take? Are there other clients waiting? Did my emotional outburst earlier throw us off schedule? I hope I'm not taking up too much time.*

Sensing her tension, he asked her to take three deep breaths, as they had done before. "Quiet your mind and concentrate on your breathing. Fill your lungs with the clean, pure air and feel the gentle rise and fall of your body's breath." His voice was slow, smooth and almost hypnotic. As she felt each breath rhythmically move in and out of her body, gradually her mind cleared and she became focused on her breathing, allowing her to be fully present in the moment, with each inhalation and exhalation.

During the Tui Na treatment, her muscles were pounded and pressure points pushed as she relaxed to a level she couldn't remember ever being at before. Anytime she felt pain, as the muscles disobediently tried to cling to their knots, she took a deep breath, like she had done before, and her body relaxed further into a sense of serenity. She was almost asleep at the end and struggled to get up when it was time to leave.

Speaking seemed unnecessary and as she stood up she experienced a wave of dizziness. She felt a strange sense of perspective, which she couldn't put into words, realising that her body was the greatest object she owned and she needed to look after it. She felt emotional, but not like she wanted to cry, just like a strong energy was searing through her. She thanked Dr Wu, agreed to another appointment the following day and quietly left by the same doors she had bounded through earlier that day.

She felt like she was floating in a dream as she walked home in the last of the evening sun. She could smell the plants, the flowers and spicy flavours in the wind as people cooked their dinners. She heard the insects busy in the hedgerow and the beautiful chirping of the evening birdsongs overhead. She felt an excited yet content energy that took her home with a light spring in her step.

She slept very well that night. She fell asleep at eight o'clock and awoke the following morning at ten thirty, amazed at the amount her body had rested. She didn't even get to see Pam, to tell her about her experiences, as Pam had come home and left again for work whilst she was asleep.

***

Jessica went back to the holistic health centre at two o'clock, the time they had agreed and Dr Wu was there to greet her. His smiling eyes penetrated deep into her, like a hug for the soul.

"You seem a lot more relaxed today," he said as she walked in. "Stress is a messenger to tell you that something needs to change."

He suggested that they do some yoga, and she admitted that she had never tried it before but was happy to give it a go. Jessica had so many vouchers she was happy to try any of the courses, even if she didn't really know what she was doing.

They went deep into the garden beyond the

courtyard and up some steps to a type of wooden tree house, looking out onto the top of the trees. Intense incense caught in Jessica's throat as the smoke danced in front of her and then cleared. Dr Wu asked her to lie down on one of the two blue yoga mats, which were laid side by side. Like the day before, they started with breathing exercises, taking long deep breaths in and out and becoming conscious of each breath and how it was moving through the body.

Dr Wu gently led her through a series of yoga poses, guiding her with his voice as his body showed her what to do. Jessica followed the movements, connecting in unison with each position.

"Focus on the trees," he said, looking out the window, as he tucked his left foot to rest on his right thigh and she followed to take on the 'tree' yoga position. "The trees give in to the gentle movements of the winds above, their grounding and roots of foundation run deep within the earth…"

Jessica tried to concentrate on what he was saying as she wobbled from side to side.

I'm more like a blooming tree being felled, she thought, as she toppled over. She began with the easiest position, just balancing her foot against her other ankle, before moving it up to her calf and finally her thigh. It took her a while but she stabilised, centred herself and was able to reconnect with Dr Wu's words.

"You are just like the tree," he continued, remaining calm and still, seemingly unfazed by her comical air flapping and continual falling over. "Your heart pumps life through branches of veins, which extend throughout your body. The trunk of the tree is like your core. You must dig deep roots to find support and sustenance, so that your tree can flourish and be at one with nature."

It took her a while to stop laughing as she continued to wobble, but as the sun shone through the branches of the trees outside, she started to feel a sense of connection through Dr Wu's words to the nature all around her. Finally she was still and centred. The more he spoke, the more it intrigued her and the more it started to make sense in her mind. Although she had no balance to begin with, she trusted in his coaching and began to feel stronger and more centred as they progressed.

Chapter Eight

"You what?" shouted Pam over the pounding sound system in the pub, which had got busier and louder as their Saturday afternoon catch up turned into a busy Saturday night. "He touched you where?" She laughed as she drained the last of her glass of wine.

As hard as she tried, Jessica didn't seem to be able to explain her experiences with Dr Wu at the retreat centre. "He… I mean, Dr Wu… opened my chakras and realigned my Qi," she said laughing uncertainly, not really knowing if she had got it right and realising how crazy it sounded coming out of her mouth.

"He opened your… chee? Ooh-err missus. Sounds a bit rude to me," Pam laughed. "You're sounding well drunk. You're away with the fairies. I didn't have you down as a hippy." They both laughed as Pam pulled Jessica towards the bar yet again and decided to start ordering shots. Jessica knew she was in for a big night.

Tranquillity and calmness were forgotten as Pam and Jessica could no longer hear each other over the music, which had gradually got louder until all they could do was merrily dance instead. On the next round to the bar they had to queue behind a large group of lively men.

"Get us a drink," Pam shouted to one of the men at the front.

"What's it worth?" he said, giving Pam a huge smile, which seemed to catch her attention, as she smiled back.

"Well that depends…" she flirted, leaving the sentence lingering in the air.

Sensing his luck was in, he bought them their drinks and then ordered a round of shots for the group, including the two girls.

Suzie and Emma turned up for the 'prowl' evening Pam had arranged, looking incredibly glamorous, with immaculate hair and make-up, wearing dresses they had borrowed from Pam. Jessica tried to talk to the other girls, but the music was so loud that even when they were shouting at full volume, she could only make out every other word. There wasn't much chance of having a conversation; the only option was to dance. By that time in the evening, it was all about looks and body language and Jessica felt very scruffy in her day wear, faded jeans and T shirt, surrounded by all the beautiful women in their 'party pulling dresses'. Her solution was to drink through it until she felt confident and didn't care anymore, lost in the music and the movement. Their quiet lunchtime drink turned into a full-on Saturday night and Jessica became part of a large group of guys and girls, dancing and doing multiple shots. Pam seemed particularly keen on 'the hunk' as she called him, who she had met at the bar and encouraged to buy them lots of drinks. At the end of the night, Jessica helped Suzie and Emma flag down a taxi home, then had to drag Pam away from 'the hunk' who she was kissing outside the pub. It was the lure of kebabs that finally convinced Pam to leave and walk home with Jessica.

"I've got his number." Pam proudly showed Jessica as they meandered arm in arm down the street, Pam stopping to wave to her 'hunk' as she wobbled home.

"Are you going to call him?" enquired Jessica.

"I'm not sure. Maybe. Hey, thanks for making me leave. Yes, I've got to be more ladylike…" said Pam, bursting out laughing. "By getting a kebab!"

"I thought you were going to have him for breakfast," Jessica teased.

"It was only a kiss," Pam said dismissively. "A kiss means nothing at all! A kebab, however, that means everything." She laughed as she skipped off down the street to the kebab house on their way home.

* * *

Jessica woke up the next afternoon, with a pounding headache and a very fuzzy memory of the night before. Any movement, however small, sent her into a whirlwind of pain and spinning, making her feel very sick. So she lay as still as she could, trying to work out what had happened the night before and piece it altogether.

She thought back, trying to explain her experiences at the pub and Pam's dismissal of her new interests.

She couldn't describe what had happened to her at the holistic centre in a way that made sense to the outside world. She felt torn between her old sense of self, of working and drinking to forget the work, and her new self-discovery and how renewed and alive she had felt with Dr Wu at the centre. She thought about what Dr Wu would have made of their drunken behaviour last night and felt conflicted.

Am I crazy? Jessica started to doubt herself. *Maybe I should just stop all this nonsense now, start focusing on getting a job? Yoga and meditation is all very well, but it's not going to sound great on my CV, or pay the bills! Maybe Pam is right and it's all a load of hippy nonsense?*

A silent tear fell from her eye and she noticed its warmth turn cold as it trickled down her cheek. Then she realised she was going to be sick and ran full speed to the bathroom. She spent the day in bed feeling very unwell, caught in a hazy space between two worlds.

* * *

When Jessica turned up at the centre for her session on Monday she had to wait while Dr Wu finished off with another client. She sat in the white reception area, nestling into the scatter cushions trying to get comfortable, thinking back to the first time she had bounded through the doors. Just then, Dr Wu came out of his room with an attractive girl who was giggling and touching Dr Wu's arm with fondness as she thanked him. She was in her early to mid-twenties and looked very fit, wearing tight trousers and a figure-hugging top, with blond curls bouncing down her back. They both leant in to bow, with their hands held together at their hearts, like in prayer, and said 'Namaste' to each other. The lady then whooshed out of the centre oblivious to Jessica and her comfortable little space that she thought she had carved out as her own.

A strange feeling started in Jessica's stomach and spread throughout every vein in her body. She couldn't place it. Like a mixture of frustration and sadness, like she wanted to scream, cry or kick something in anger.

"Who was that?" Jessica said scornfully to Dr Wu, like a married woman who has just found her husband having an affair. She had no idea why she was feeling jealous.

"She's a yoga teacher, she came in for a treatment and is interested in teaching a class here," he said in his usual friendly tone.

"I don't think she would fit in here," she said sternly. "She's too… noisy. I mean, she's not someone I would want to do yoga with!" She surprised herself at her own assertion as she walked into Dr Wu's room and sat down on the chair. She knew she must seem ridiculous but she couldn't yet control her raging emotions, even though rationally she didn't understand why she was even feeling them.

"What's the matter, Jessica?" Dr Wu's soft tone and kind inflection melted and thawed the icy atmosphere. "Ouch! Your energy is all spiky and sharp, like claws, what's up?"

"Nothing," she said, almost in a teenage sulk, slumped over in her chair.

"I think we need to work on your heart chakra today, the anahata, which translates to 'unhurt'. It sits in the middle of your seven chakras, connecting the physical and spiritual and is the source of love and compassion. Blockages can lead to feelings of jealousy, fear of betrayal and anger towards others. Opening and unblocking the anahata chakra allows pure love to flow, opening your heart to others and to new experiences, allowing you to fully know what's in your heart. Love has the highest frequency of energy and if we are full of love then we are full of life."

Before she had a chance to say anything, he leant forwards, took her hands in his and pulled her towards him so she was sitting upright.

God, his hands are soft and warm and lovely, she thought, as her heart started to pound in her chest. He placed her hands on her knees, came behind her and pushed her back forward and shoulders back, to straighten her spine, so she was sitting straight with her feet firmly on the floor.

"Deep breaths in through the nose, and out through the mouth, in… out… in… out… good." It was like hypnotherapy, she already felt the state of relaxation creep over her whole body.

"Every breath in is fresh, clean, renewing energy, each breath out releases stress, tension, and any negative energy. Let it go. Keep breathing…" He was hardly touching her, but it felt like his voice was deep inside her, massaging every muscle, hugging her heart. Her mind cleared and she was in the moment, only aware of her body and breath. She found herself in her new world of peace, calm and serenity once again.

* * *

On Friday night when Pam wanted to go out clubbing to 'escape and obliterate all memories of the week', Jessica politely declined. She realised that she no longer wanted to 'escape' her life, she actually wanted to embrace it. Instead of trying to lose her mind, through drinking, she wanted to find it. She surprised herself by how much better she felt staying in, reading and relaxing, without any of the former fear of missing out that she had always felt if she had not gone out drinking at the weekend.

On Saturday she went to pick up her parents' old carriage clock that she had taken in to be repaired. She was delighted to find it as good as new, in fact it had been so well polished that it sparkled like she'd never seen before.

She proudly placed it back in the centre of the mantelpiece in her bedroom and felt a strong positive connection, a gratitude for its very existence, rather than the sadness she had previously felt when she had looked at it. It had a slight mark, a scar, down the side of the wood, but Jessica knew that would remind her of how precious it was and how time now took on a new meaning for her.

Chapter Nine

Hours became days, and days became weeks, visiting the centre every day. Time seemed to blur, becoming insignificant to the moments of meaning Dr Wu gave her. Bursts of insight beaded together, like unique pearls softly reflecting the light of life around them, held together on the string of time. The construct of time that had bound her so tightly, somehow became immaterial to the pearls of wisdom beautifying the delicacy of creation.

She wasn't sure how many vouchers she had left, she had given them all across at the beginning of her sessions and asked the nice Chinese lady to let her know when she was running out, which she expected must be soon.

Jessica had been so tightly wound that it took her a while to fully relax and calm her chattering mind. Dr Wu used visualisation exercises to channel her energy in an inward exploration of her deeper consciousness and purpose.

"Meditation is the journey of the mind," Dr Wu said, during one of their sessions, lying on the mat in the tree house after their yoga. "Travel through time, space and your own limitations. Go wherever you want, be whomever you want, do whatever you want, the only limit is your imagination."

She felt a positive charge run through her veins and her arms got goosebumps although she wasn't cold. The fine hairs on her arms stood up and her spine tingled as her body lightly shivered and shuddered. His words connected deeply, causing this physical reaction to cascade through her whole body as she drank in his voice.

"The human being is a very complex and fascinating creature," he continued, "with powers well beyond its understanding, living in a world far more complex than can be conceived or controlled." She closed her eyes and let his wisdom wash over her, absorbing meaning at the deepest level.

"Imagine if I told you I could transport you to the life of your dreams. Are you ready to embark on a journey of deep discovery to the most amazing places imaginable?"

The voice whispered soft, smooth and almost inaudible. Did she actually hear it or was she just dreaming?

Slightly dizzy with oxygen, breathing deep into her lungs, Jessica relaxed into the ground around her, melting into the floor. Her thoughts slipped from colours, shapes and movements to a warm white light centring her stillness.

"When you open your mind, your imagination, what do you see, hear, feel, smell? You can be anywhere… be anything you can imagine…"

With her eyes closed and body resting, she started to feel the soft onset of a sleepy dreamlike state, yet

An Invitation . . . To the Life of Your Dreams

with an astute awareness within her. Like a daydream, she understood that she could control the journey she was about to take.

If I can transport myself anywhere, where do I want to go? Who do I want to be? she thought, as she drifted into her imagination.

She visualised waking up in an airy room on a large bed with soft white sheets, wooden floors and bright and airy French windows, letting in warm sparkling sunlight. Through the double doors was a wide terrace, where a table was laid with a continental breakfast, a vast array of fresh fruits, pastries, yogurt and muesli. She could smell fresh coffee and taste the aroma of blueberries and strawberries lightly roasted in the sun. She walked over to the edge of the terrace to look out onto the most amazing view. A valley of green trees and flowering shrubs stretched to the sea, where she could see yachts and sailing boats. She felt so alive, so full of possibilities. She wasn't sure if it was his voice infiltrating her mind, but just then Dr Wu came to her side on the terrace, looking at the view with her. In a half dreamlike state, caught between her visualisation and the reality of the yoga room, she could hear his breathing, the softness of his whispering words on her mind.

It was at that moment that she felt a heavy blanket of mystery lift off her. She realised that she was in control of her life, her journey, her destiny. She could go anywhere, do anything, be anyone, both in the dream and in reality.

It was at the end of this meditation that she made a conscious choice to go from existing to living. She thought of all the hundreds of faces that she saw every day, each with their own story, their own purpose and their own journey. Yet many of those people were drifting through life in a trance, sleep-walking through their reality, too busy to stop and notice life, and all its unlimited possibilities, all around them. She felt enlightened, realising that life is to be lived, with purpose, passion and a connection to other people.

***

With the guidance of Dr Wu over the sessions, her yoga and meditation got stronger and she no longer felt conscious of herself or the wobbles of imbalance. She felt safe with Dr Wu as though she were connected to something much greater than herself.

Through yoga, she saluted the sun, grounded herself in the tree pose and took time to connect with her body, breath and surroundings, curling up in restorative poses to let her mind drift. The more she relaxed and accessed her inner self, the deeper she journeyed into her dreams.

During the massage one Thursday afternoon, she lost herself in the moment, the movement and the music. Dr Wu encouraged her to explore visual images that came into her mind and drift into them.

"Let yourself go to wherever you want to go. Imagine you are on a journey of deep discovery, venture deep into your heart, your inner creative, your imagination. What is it telling you? What is it showing you?" Dr Wu's voice comforted her like a soft security blanket, wrapping her up safely in relaxation and comfort.

The gentle Chinese music, with faint bells, strings and exotic woodwind instruments, made a soft soothing melody, like spirits dancing in the breeze of a deep forest. The music infiltrated her imagination and placed itself as a representation in her mind as she drifted off to a foreign land. She could see a wide arching tree on top of a rock on the side of a mountain. A girl was sitting in the shade beneath the tree, blowing into a small musical instrument, sending the beautiful melody out across the distance. The commanding views of nature, mountains and trees made the silhouette of the girl seem tiny, yet her music carried great distances, reaching far beyond her existence like a timeless soul.

Jessica could almost feel the breeze tickling her skin, smell the green earthy smell of damp foliage and mud, feel the rocks and sand under her feet. She thought about how stunningly beautiful nature was, as she looked at the harmony of this vivid picture in her mind and how everything was interconnected. The mountain was strong, solid, commanding and immovable. The impermeable rock she stood on in her mind was thick, cold and deep. The soft dust, which lay on the ground, had once been part of the mountain, yet was tiny in comparison and had no such commanding strength. However, the tiny particles could collectively amount to a great mass or roam free, dancing on the winds, travelling with the music that reached far into the distance.

"Wake up. Wake up…" Jessica could hear a soft

voice coming through the breeze of the mountain. For a moment she wondered if it was the mountain itself talking to her. Then she recognised Dr Wu's voice, had he come to find her? She felt a positive energy of consciousness rise and then, with a start, she was back in the room.

Awakening from her journey, momentarily unsure of where she was, it was a surprise to be on the bed in the holistic centre and not actually on a mountain in another land far away. It had felt so real, so intense. She looked at Dr Wu slightly confused, starting to question what was real and what was a dream.

"I, err… I must have fallen asleep," she slurred, getting up and trying to wipe away any possible dribble from her dry mouth. "I was dreaming, but it really felt real, really… real!"

"Then it was real. Real to your subconscious anyway."

"My dream was real?" she exclaimed slowly, unsure if she had misheard him. "What do you mean?" She felt sleepy and confused, her mind misty, half awake and half asleep.

"Our brains operate on different levels," he explained, as she came round and her senses returned to the room. "If we can control our thoughts, then we control the perceptions of our experience. Reality is just the perception we create in our mind."

"I had very strong visualisations of a place, a specific view from a mountain. I have never been there. I don't even know if it's a real place, so how could it have felt so real, so clear in my mind?" Jessica exclaimed, unsettled.

An Invitation ... To the Life of Your Dreams

"We perceive so many things, we are only aware of some of them consciously. Our subconscious, however, is constantly absorbing and taking in information all by itself, so it is possible that you may have come across this image before but not been aware of it. Our deeper subconscious mind does not differentiate between real and perceived, so it believes everything is real. Have you ever felt physically scared watching a horror movie, or cried at a sad film, even though you know it is not real?"

She nodded, rubbing away the chills that shivered down her arms.

"You have journeyed to a place deep within your soul, transported by your heart and mind," he said as he sat down next to her, gently placing his hand on her shoulder. "By harmonising your body, breath and thoughts, you are awaking your spirit and unlocking desires that are deep within you."

Her body felt alive, like electricity was being pumped through her, she felt the intensity of the moment: her heart, her breath, the heat of Dr Wu's hand on her shoulder, ripples of warm energy cascading down her arm and into her chest.

"When you awaken from within, you know who you are and the unique gifts you have to share with the world. Then you can make any dream come true. Listen to your heart, your intuition, or inner guidance, to discover what is meaningful to you and then become it. Live your life on purpose."

Just then she did something that she didn't understand, which would stay with her for the rest of her life. She didn't know why, she didn't know what came over her, and no amount of questioning or reasoning could explain it to her. But, just then, without any conscious thought, she leant forward and kissed Dr Wu, kissed him so passionately and with such penetration that he couldn't have pulled away even if he had wanted to.

He knew he couldn't have pulled away, even if the shock of the situation hadn't paralysed him to stay in her embrace, in the brief moment when their bodies connected physically, as well as emotionally and spiritually. Or that may have been just what he told himself, how he justified to himself why he hadn't pulled away, why he let the kiss linger longer. Why their bodies had stayed locked, linked through soft moist lips, inhaling each other's breath, sharing an intense and intimate moment. He was surprised by himself, by how much he wanted this woman. By how connected he felt to her. How could he have let himself develop such strong feelings? He was always so professional, so studious; he didn't entertain the idea of female courtship, preferring to focus his attention on his work and his studies. He knew that his parents back in China would let him know when was the right time to marry, once he had proved himself as an international doctor. They would have a large part to play in determining the appropriate suitor for their successful son living and working in London.

Jessica felt the connection to the man who had given her so much, allowing her to uncover her true self and grow from within as a person. However, she also saw the look of confusion in his eyes, as they momentarily locked into each other's senses, and she suddenly felt overwhelmed and ashamed to have put him in a difficult position. She pulled away, lowering her face, apologising and pulling herself together.

"I am your teacher," was all he said, as he stood up quietly and walked outside.

Jessica collected her things together, steadying herself as she smoothed her hair down, and with a deep breath she walked out into the main reception. Dr Wu was nowhere in sight, she thought that he must have gone through the leafy arch deep into the gardens. No one else was around. Everything was still and silent. Jessica put on her coat and left, feeling embarrassed and confused. She had not meant to compromise her teacher. She had never thrown herself at anyone like that. She could not come back tomorrow or, in fact, ever again.

Chapter Ten

Jessica wanted to keep her mind busy, to forget about Dr Wu, to forget about what she had done. She thought back to Pam and 'the hunk', when Pam had said that a kiss meant nothing, but this kiss had meant everything to Jessica. It had changed everything.

With no therapy to focus on, she was in danger of being dragged into negative thoughts again as her reality hit her: *I have no job, no relationship, no one to talk to and I still don't even know where Bruce is. Bruce!* she thought with a sudden sense of purpose and determination, *I need to find out what has happened to him.*

Seizing her phone she dialled the switchboard for work and after a number of rings Anita finally answered.

"Anita, hi it's Jessica. I need to know…"

"Hello Jessica, how are you?" Anita sounded tired and launched into her script before Jessica even had a chance to say anything else. "I understand that you want to know what is going on, everyone does. The board are still working on everything at the moment. You will continue to be paid your full salary for now and they are finalising packages as we speak."

"Thanks Anita, that's good to know, but…" started Jessica.

"I know it's an unsettling time, but don't worry, it will all be sorted out soon," Anita continued, as if reciting the same thing for the hundredth time.

"Thanks, I appreciate that, but…" Jessica persisted. She could hear three or four other phone lines all ringing around Anita.

"Anita, I know this must be crazy busy for you and I am sorry that you have to put up with everyone asking you questions all day, I imagine it must be really difficult. I know you want to get off the phone to answer the next call but just give me a minute."

"Sure, yes, sorry Jess, it's crazy manic here," said Anita, she seemed to warm slightly, connecting to Jessica as a person rather than just another employee harassing her.

"In fact, Jess, and I shouldn't really say this, but I know that you are in a very strong position, they have taken your loyal service and proximity to the sensitivity of the situation into consideration. I can assure you that the payout they are proposing will be to your advantage."

"Thanks Anita, that's really good to hear. Listen, I actually phoned up to ask about Bruce. Have you heard from him? Do you know where he is or how I can get hold of him?" Jessica finally blurted out without interruption.

"Er… no, no I have not!" Anita sounded cold and abrupt again, taking a deep breath before continuing. "We are not allowed to give out personal information or contact details. You know the rules. Sorry Jessica,

I really must go, it's beyond busy here. Take care of yourself and we will be sending your formal letter out very shortly. Bye." She hung up, leaving Jessica with nothing but dead air.

As Bruce's phone still didn't work, Jessica decided to drive over to his house again, this time to find that it had a sold sign outside. She knocked on the door and her heart pounded momentarily when it opened. However, it was a young man standing before her who had apparently bought the house directly through the estate agents and had never even met Bruce.

"For a VERY good price too," boasted the tall young man who now owned Bruce's house. "It's such a shame that these things happen," he said, with no genuine emotion or care. "Divorce hey, it's a nasty thing. Good for me as I got a bargain, but nasty for the people who had to sell the house in a hurry. At least there were no kids involved," he added, as if that made it all ok. He rooted through a folder of documents and gave her a new contact number to try, which Jessica noticed had a strange combination of numbers at the beginning. Wishing her luck, in a polite but now-leave-me-alone kind of way, the new owner closed the door on Jessica and her search for Bruce, disappearing into what was now his new home and his life.

How fickle it all is, Jessica thought as she drove back home and confined herself to the safety of her room. *We think these things are so important: our home, our lives, our work, but it's all so superficial. Meaningless.*

She focused on typing in the correct sequence of

numbers as she started calling the phone number she'd been given. *Bruce can't have just disappeared into thin air. There's got to be more to it. I've got to get to the bottom of this.*

Eventually, on the eighth attempted call that evening, Bruce finally answered.

"Hello…? HELLO!" Bruce shouted aggressively down the crackly line, sounding agitated, his voice rough and grouchy.

"Bruce?" replied Jessica rather sheepishly. "Bruce, is that you?"

"Yes it's Bruce, who the bloody hell is this?"

She wondered if he was drunk, if he had become addicted to drugs, if he had become homeless or was in temporary accommodation somewhere. Her thoughts filled her with a sickening fear as she tried to sound cheery, making her voice come out all high pitched and squeaky. Her heart was pounding in her ears and she could hardly breathe.

"It's Jessica. Bruce, are you ok? I've been so worried. Where are you?"

"Jessica? Jess, is that you?" he sounded genuinely delighted as he recognised her.

"Yes, it's me. Are you ok? I was worried."

"Hi Jess, yes I am fine thanks, despite being woken up by constant phone calls! What time is it?"

Woken up? she thought. *There must be something wrong if he's fast asleep at this time.*

"It's eight in the evening, Bruce!"

"It's three in the morning here in China and yes, I was asleep. I'll call you later." His tone of voice told Jessica to let him go back to sleep and not ask any more questions. She felt relieved that he was alive and well.

"China? Oh, ok. Yes, of course. Sorry to wake you. I'm so pleased you're all right. I hope you sleep well and I…" And with that the phone line dropped and she was left with silence and then pips.

At least he's alive, she thought, feeling relieved. *Bruce obviously needs me. Listen to him, he sounds awful. I am going to be there for him. I am going to help.*

This sense of duty made her feel needed again, giving her a sense of purpose, allowing her to focus on other people's lives rather than her own. She poured herself a large glass of wine, feeling pleased and relieved to have something else to think about. Feeling a strange mixture of emotions and relief, she poured herself a second glass of wine and then a third. She thought of Bruce with warm affection, delighted to know that he was all right and in China of all places.

She thought about his dark brooding looks and wide white smile, which released his booming laugh that filled the room. He had a strange hold over her she couldn't explain. It was as if she had hidden herself and her identity in a need to serve him and be seen as worthy in his eyes. For years, she had given him her all, poured all her energy into this man. She didn't know if it was love, lust or just admiration. Perhaps it was actually a deep insecurity she had projected onto him as a figure of authority, after blocking out all her emotions from her parents' accident, for which she blamed herself. Whilst Jessica didn't understand all the emotions flowing through her, along with the wine, she just felt a comforting sense of familiarity with Bruce that she could hold onto.

* * *

It was Bruce's turn to wake Jessica up who was completely out of it when he called. She had managed to polish off a whole bottle of wine that evening and when Pam had come home around ten thirty that night, they had opened a second. So when Bruce called Jessica at eight in the morning, she was fast asleep and disorientated.

Jessica heard the phone but it took her some time to realise that she needed to wake up from her dreams in order to answer the call. Her head pounded and the room was spinning all around her. When she saw the name 'Bruce' come up on her mobile's display, she forgot that she had only just added the contact the night before and it instantly took her back to her old world of work, when Bruce had often called her in the middle of the night with some emergency or another.

"Bruce? What is it? What's the matter? Is it work?" She burst out as she eventually came around from her sleep and answered the phone in a mild panic.

"Work? What? No. It's me Jess, it's Bruce. How the devil are you?" He sounded much jollier than on their last call.

"Hi Bruce," she paused, unsure of what to say. Her head was swimming in the darkness of the room and her red wine induced sleep.

"Have I woken you up? Sorry, Jess. I'm getting my own back for last night, I couldn't wait to call you. How's everything with you?"

"I'm fine," Jessica lied and quickly tried to relinquish her end of the conversation. "How are you?"

Luckily that was enough to get Bruce going, and he talked non-stop all about going to China and what he was doing. He told Jessica about how he had decided to leave everything behind and start afresh. In a sudden impulse he had gone to China on the back of a potential job offer, which had actually fallen through. He was talking about seizing the moment, not letting opportunities pass by. Jessica tried to concentrate on what he was saying, but her head felt heavy and woozy and she kept drifting in and out of sleep, occasionally throwing in "ah ha" or "uh hum" to show she was still alive and part of the conversation, which was in fact purely a monologue.

"I'm sorry I've not been in touch, Jess," he said. "Everything's been so busy and it's taken some adjusting to. Also, I've been ill, with the change in diet I think, and time just seems to have flown by without me even realising it."

Jessica thought he sounded a bit different, possibly more relaxed.

"So when are you coming over to China?" Bruce said with a cheeky sound to his voice. Jessica knew she had been asked a question but couldn't quite process it.

"Err...?" was all Jessica could muster.

"Oh come on Jess, it'll be great. You'll love it,

there's so much to see and do. Come and stay with me? We'll have a blast. Say yes Jess, say you'll come?"

"Err…" Jessica repeated, her mind still swimming in last night's red wine. "Yes…?" she said tentatively, not really sure what she was saying but just agreeing with Bruce, as she always did.

"Excellent! Oh, that's such good news, Jess, I'll look into flights and send some over today, I've got loads of air miles you can use. It'll be quick to get your visa too, I know a guy who can help, I'll get him to sort it for you. Great, I will see you very soon. Let me know when it's booked." He was excited and full of life; Jessica couldn't help laughing out loud and feeling excited too.

"It's great to hear you sounding so jolly again, Bruce," Jessica said fondly, thinking back to his assertive determined nature at work, which was what she had loved so much about him. Somehow it made her feel safe, having someone tell her what to do. She didn't have responsibility for making decisions anymore, for trying to work out her own mind. If she didn't have responsibility then she couldn't mess it all up, could she? Bruce was back and he would sort it out for her. She put the phone down and drifted back into a deep sleep.

* * *

That afternoon Jessica woke with a terrible headache. Her body ached all over and her mouth felt like the bottom of a birdcage. She groaned as she struggled out of bed to the bathroom and had to stop in the doorway and hold on tight as her head spun round, so dizzy she thought she might fall over. After a slow start, forcing herself to eat dry toast, washed down with strong black coffee, she eventually found herself at the computer checking emails. There were seven emails from Bruce. She read the top one in her inbox, which was the last one he had sent and nearly leapt from her seat.

> Good news, I've spoken to Jonny, and it's all good to go. He's going to get your visa sorted in the next couple of days and says it will be in good time for the Tuesday flight, so I've booked it for you. AMEX had all your passport information from previous business trips, which was lucky, and I just used some of my millions of air miles - bonus! Can't wait to see you, lots of love, Bruce X

"WHAT?" Jessica shouted out loud. "Tuesday? But that's only a few days away. I don't... err?" Realising she was talking out loud to herself she stopped talking and started looking through the email trail, trying to put the pieces of the jigsaw together.

Whilst she had been asleep, Bruce seemed to have spent the day sorting out her trip. He had started with options in the first email, with each email after that getting more and more manic and excited, having a conversation with himself resulting in the decision being made for her. Jessica hadn't been awake to be the calming rational influence on his manic episodes, as she always used to be. She had always made him take a moment to stop and think before acting on impulse, something he was very quick to do.

As Jessica sat paralysed in her seat at the computer, Pam came home. She took one look at Jessica, who was still in her pyjamas with bed hair and bad breath, staring in disbelief at her computer and laughed.

"Whoa girl, I think you drunk too much last night. Look at the state of you." Pam fanned her nose from the smell and went straight to the window to let in some fresh air.

"I'm going to China," Jessica blurted out, "on Tuesday!"

"What? China? Why?" Pam stopped still, tilting her head at Jessica as if to hear correctly.

"Bruce!" Jessica said, as if that answered everything. She wanted to explain about the emails, but didn't know where to start and didn't think Pam would understand.

"Bruce? You mean your old boss Bruce? He's turned up at last then?" Pam spat. Jessica could sense that Pam was growing more irritated by the second. She knew that Pam didn't trust Bruce one bit and didn't like Jessica's subservience to him.

"Yes, he's in China and he's booked me a ticket to go on Tuesday to visit. I…" Jessica could hear the words coming out and knew it sounded crazy, but she didn't have the energy to fight it.

"Are you sure you know what you are doing, Jess?" said Pam. "It seems a bit sudden. What happened to Dr Wu and your hippy holistic stuff, I thought you were enjoying that?"

"It's fine. I'm not doing that any more. I am going to China on Tuesday."

"Are you ok, Jess? What's happened to you recently, you were all calm and zen and then, bam, you're all over the place again?" she asked with concern.

"I'm FINE!" Jessica snapped and then immediately felt bad. "Sorry!" she added before getting up and slipping off to her room sheepishly, hiding herself under her duvet and hoping for the day to be over.

Even though she wouldn't admit it to her, Pam had noticed a positive change in Jessica since she had been going to the holistic health and wellbeing centre. She had noticed that she seemed happier, calm, grounded and content. However, it seemed to Pam that Jessica had suddenly relapsed back to the frantic obsessive person who dropped everything for their boss, and she wasn't sure why.

* * *

Over the next few days, Jessica's world turned upside down as did her bedroom, which was all over the place. She filled her time and mind frantically rushing around getting her visa, having inoculations, buying items and packing her cases. She was used to travelling with work; often having to drop everything and fly off to business meetings at very little notice, so she got back into work mode, focusing on being efficient and effective with packing and preparing the necessary requirements, without pausing to actually ask herself what she was doing and why.

Pam was right that Jessica seemed to have reverted to her old pattern of behaviour, replacing her feelings and emotions with urgent errands and stressful business. Jessica convinced herself that she didn't have time to think about anything, she had too much to do. Every time Dr Wu crept into her mind, or anything relating to the calm peaceful serenity she had felt at the centre, she would try and snap her mind out of the thoughts and replace them with things to do. She pushed herself until she was exhausted and when she woke up in the middle of the night and couldn't sleep, she would make lists and do research and organise the trip, anything to avoid allowing her mind the space to think and reflect.

Jessica knew she was not being rational, but she was afraid of her own thoughts and feelings. As she bundled her suitcases into the back of a taxi on Tuesday morning, Pam tried one last time to talk her round.

"Are you sure you want to do this, Jess?" Pam sighed. "You seem a bit stressed. It's all a bit of a rush. Would it not be better to wait and…"

"Pam, I've told you, it's fine," Jessica said firmly, trying to close down the conversation. She heaved her suitcase off the curb and the driver helped her with it into the taxi.

"But… You… " Pam stuttered, at a loss for what to say.

"Thanks Pam, it's ok, it's all sorted. I'll still pay the rent, so there's nothing to worry about."

"I'm not worried about the rent," Pam said, although she was secretly relieved to hear that. "I'm worried about you. This trip to China, it's all happened very quickly. When are you coming back?"

"I don't know. It doesn't matter. I'll let you know when I'm out there. I'll keep in touch by email," she said, as she slid into the back seat and grabbed for the door.

"See you later, Pam. Bye." She closed the door and the taxi pulled away. Just like that she was gone. Pam stood in the street in her dressing gown and slippers, dazed. Jessica felt bad that she had been short with Pam when she suggested that she should wait a while and prepare herself properly to go to China. In reality, Jessica knew deep down that Pam was probably right. However, instead she dismissed her concern, and tried to turn the negative feelings she had into positive ones, as she had practised in the centre. *I am free, able to go off on adventures whenever I want,* she told herself. *I've never been to China before and I am going to enjoy it. Here's to the adventure.*

Chapter Eleven

Unable to sleep on the thirteen-hour flight, Jessica had nowhere to go, nothing to do to distract her, she had to face up to herself. She suddenly caught up with her frantic behaviour, the whirlwind of activity and everything she had done to avoid thinking about kissing Dr Wu.

Jessica felt awful about pushing Pam away, just as she had pushed away all her friends after university, after what happened to her parents. Back then Jessica had convinced herself that she didn't have time for friends with her busy work.

What excuse do I have now? she thought. *I do really appreciate Pam's friendship and how she helped me when I was so down. She deserves better.* She vowed to write to her from China and get her a nice gift when she came home, although she wasn't sure when that would be. She had an open ticket and tourist visa valid for three months. She was still on full pay and she knew she had a financial payment package coming her way soon, so she could continue to pay her rent by direct debit and didn't need to rush into finding another job for the time being.

Am I crazy to drop everything, not that I have much to

drop, and go chasing after my boss, or ex-boss, travelling across the world? she thought, suspecting that the answer was in fact 'yes' and half smiled. *After all the years we've spent together, it's natural to miss him and miss being needed isn't it?* She tried to rationalise her behaviour but it still somehow didn't seem quite right to her, deep down in her tummy she felt unsettled and uncertain.

Hearing from Bruce again had given her a sense of comfort and familiarity. She had spent years working closely with Bruce and they had been through so much together. She had probably spent more time with Bruce than anyone else, including Steve her ex-(nearly)fiancé. Sometimes Bruce had joked with Jessica that they might as well have been an old married couple. She had deeply admired him and respected him, trying to prove herself to him within the company, and he had been a role model, who she set high on a grand pedestal.

She felt sorry for him and everything that he had been going through on his own, and she felt a little upset that he had not confided in her and told her about his wife leaving him. *Now that he is no longer my boss and is getting divorced, will things be different?* she caught herself wondering. Then her thoughts returned to Dr Wu and his kind understanding of her. A scurrying nervousness filled her chest. She felt sick. She was alone, leaving behind everything she knew and everyone she had known. Unsure of herself or where she was going, she couldn't sit still and couldn't supress her thoughts anymore. She wanted to turn back, to go home and back to Dr Wu and the centre, but it was too late.

Pam was right, she thought. *This is not rational behaviour. What am I doing? Am I breaking free of my past and following my heart, or just running away from it? I don't know anymore.* She felt lost and confused by her own mind and totally alone, even though she was confined to a small space with lots of people around her. An elderly French couple, who didn't seem to speak a word of English, sat next to her. They seemed so in love and so happy, as they sat hand in hand, asleep, resting against each other. Her heart felt heavy, despite the excitement of the adventure ahead. She plugged in the airline headphones to drown out her thoughts, half watching movies to distract herself.

* * *

Arriving in China, with no sleep, it was a blur of fast moving noise, colours and smells. At the airport people kept bumping into her and then saying, "Sorry, sorry," or sometimes, "Hello? Sorry. Hello," with wide smiles and curious eyes.

Either the people here are really clumsy or they're just looking for opportunities to practise their English, she thought, as a group of three giggly girls giddily came and asked for a photo with her. *Maybe they think I am a celebrity,* she mused, as she posed with the strangers, who thanked her profusely and asked if she needed any help to which she politely declined.

Jessica had arranged to stay in a central Shanghai hotel, and to meet up with Bruce in the evening, giving her the time and space to adjust and catch up on sleep. She had a nice suited driver waving a card with her name on it at the airport, he carried her bags and treated her like royalty, as she was transferred in the luxury leather trim top of the range Mercedes to the hotel.

The drive was quite an experience! Like a white-knuckle roller-coaster ride, Jessica clung onto the seat for her life. The cars raced down the motorway at such speed, using every available space, creating lanes that didn't exist. A three-lane motorway had five lanes of traffic, all going at top speed, skilfully avoiding the cars that were merely inches from each other. Once in the city, the entourage of bicycles weaving into every tiny available space was crazy. The sheer mass of people everywhere, at all times, filling all possible space, was immense.

The buildings in Shanghai were a spectrum of colours: gold, silver, red, blue, black. Huge mirrored glass structures, a building that looked like a pineapple with crowns, and buildings that looked like birds. Jessica thought that the most amazing building of them all was the Oriental Pearl Tower. Bright pink orbs hung from a triangular structure with a glass lift travelling through a shaft into the pink balls. It looked like something from another world, like something from a science fiction movie; the city was like a backdrop for a film set of the future. It didn't seem real. Jessica's senses were so overwhelmed with the variety of new and different experiences that it felt like she was in a dream.

Arriving at the hotel and finally closing the door

on the vastness of life outside, Jessica locked herself into the clean, white minimal room. She tucked the white sheets on the super comfortable bed around her and fell into a deep dreamless sleep, exhausted.

* * *

When she woke up to her alarm bleeping, it was dark and it took her a moment to realise where she was. Her mind felt fuzzy as she tried to focus her eyes and it took her a good few minutes to think about what was now her life, her reality. She heard the ticking of the clock next to her. She was no longer dreaming of China, she was actually waking up in China.

In a hazy sense of being caught between a dream and reality, which was perhaps just the jet lag, Jessica got up, washed, dressed and got ready to go and meet Bruce in the hotel bar downstairs. She painted on her make-up, transforming her dry tired face into something she thought seemed more presentable.

Downstairs, the relative grandness of the reception, with its sweeping white marble staircase, curved reception and chandelier, contrasted starkly with the small minimalistic room she had spent the last few hours sleeping in. She wasn't sure why, but she suddenly felt nervous and shy.

Am I imagining this or are all the Chinese people looking at me? And why do they then keep whispering and laughing? she thought, as she was suddenly very conscious of how far away she was from home, from her life and reality as she knew it.

She looked down and checked her cream linen

shirt-dress to make sure she hadn't spilt something. This was one of the outfits she had rushed to buy for this trip, thoughtfully selecting it for this first meeting with Bruce, to look casual, yet smart enough if he took her somewhere posh for a special dinner. It buttoned up as a high-neck dress that modestly covered her chest and shoulders and floated out as it reached her knees, with a dark brown, leather belt to tie it all together.

Self-consciously, she looked around the bar and eventually spotted the side of Bruce's head. He was sitting with three well-dressed Chinese women, who were laughing outrageously as he told jokes in animated fashion.

She walked up to them tentatively, at which point Bruce saw her and jumped out of his chair, embracing her in an elaborate over-the-top gesture, nearly spilling his strong-smelling whiskey all over her new cream dress.

"Jessica, Jessica, Jessica," he cheered loudly, hugging her again. "Welcome to China."

"Welcome to China," the chorus of Chinese ladies politely sang as they got up to leave, bowing their heads slightly before disappearing silently without trace.

"I'm sorry, where have your friends gone?" she said looking around, steadying Bruce as they sat down.

"Ah, they were just keeping me company whilst I waited for you. I've been here for a while drinking, got here early, couldn't keep my mind on anything else all day. What do you want to drink?" he said, as he shouted out for another large whiskey.

Despite the fact that Jessica was starving, they stayed

in the hotel bar all evening. Bruce didn't seem to pause for breath as he talked and talked and drank glass after glass of whiskey. Jessica didn't want to interrupt him as he poured his heart out about what had happened with his business, his wife and losing his house. Jessica sat and listened and responded with reassurance and support, as she always did.

She had been so looking forward to telling him about her experiences at the holistic centre, with the spa vouchers he had given her, but the conversation stayed on Bruce as it usually did. When he had drunk too much whiskey and could no longer talk, or walk, she kindly asked the hotel to order him a taxi and they provided a car to take him home.

This time when she returned to her room, after raiding the mini bar where she found crisps and chocolate for dinner, she desperately wanted to fall sleep, to go back to the safety of her dreams. However, her mind wouldn't let her. It seemed to race through everything she had ever thought, experienced or imagined and no matter what she tried, she couldn't stop it.

Seeing Bruce again had uncovered so many emotions. She had tried not to allow herself to feel emotion since her parents had died, keeping herself busy, preoccupied, not allowing herself to feel as it hurt too much.

She realised that she probably liked Bruce so much because he never asked her about anything personal. She could exist in a world of work, of others, where she did not have to think about herself, her life, her loss. However, this time, something had changed.

She felt annoyed that Bruce had not asked her anything about herself. He had not asked what she had been up to, or how losing her job had impacted her. He did not ask how she had used the spa vouchers he had given her, even though she had tried several times to tell him. He hadn't asked about her journey or even if she was hungry.

She realised how one-sided her relationship with Bruce was and she thought back to Dr Wu. He had always been the one to ask Jessica questions about herself, she had occasionally asked questions about him, but it had usually been all about her. She knew that he had left China at twenty-five to continue to study medicine in London, and that his parents were still in China, but she didn't even know which part of China. Ashamed, she realised that she knew very little about the man, despite feeling so connected to him. Dr Wu, who had become so central to her life and to her journey of self-discovery, the person who she felt such close connection to, was a complete mystery to her, just like her new surroundings.

That night, as she lay wide-awake listening to the unfamiliar sounds of Chinese life all around her, she vowed that she would learn more about the Chinese culture. She wanted to open her mind and heart, to break free from the trapped existence she was running away from. Her time at the holistic centre had taught her a lot, even if she hadn't realised it all yet; subliminally it had all registered in her subconscious. Somewhere deep inside she knew that she had to connect with her life's purpose and that she could no longer run or hide from it.

Chapter Twelve

The next few days were spent sightseeing with a full agenda Bruce had arranged. They were joined by a lady called Sunny, Bruce's translator and tour guide. Sunny was a beautiful Chinese woman who had long black hair, pale soft skin and a wonderful smile. She was always cheerful and went beyond helpfulness to ensure that they had everything they needed. They were spoilt with hospitality and good service everywhere they went, which was great as Jessica's jet lag was exhausting her and making everything a bit of a blur.

From the 88th floor of Jin Mao Tower, one of the tallest buildings in the world, they looked out over the top of Shanghai. The view was amazing. The city didn't look real, it was like a miniature model, with fantastic futuristic buildings dotted around. Tiny streets with tiny cars moving slowly and in formation, each denoting a central character in their own life story.

From the top, everything was in order: everything was neat and tidy and perfectly organised, a contrast to how it had felt to Jessica down in amongst it all on the ground. She thought back to what Dr Wu had said about the ripples in the pond and how we often couldn't see beyond the immediate centre where we place ourselves.

She felt a little dizzy as she looked down from the great height, and realised that she was just one of those tiny figures rushing around in their own little world. Her life could be observed as a pattern of behaviour, she was just a small part of something much bigger than herself. From the great height of perspective, the people and each of their life stories were as small as ants on a forest floor and the weight of pressure she carried seemed to lift.

When they got back on the street, the noise was deafening, cars were hooting and engines revving as the cars skimmed past each other at great speed. Crossing the road was like mission impossible. Running, jumping, dodging, tourists panicked and danced for their life across the road, much to the amusement of the locals, who could stroll through the blaring traffic seemingly with their eyes shut.

Everywhere they went, especially when they left Shanghai and ventured into the surrounding areas of China, people would stare at them. Sunny, their tour guide explained that being a foreigner in China, a 'wei guoren' (outside country person) or 'lao wei' (old outsider), attracted a lot of attention.

Sunny took them to a small village a few hours drive from Shanghai, where the whole community erupted into tears of laughter as the 'wei guoren' passed by. Small children were literally rolling around on the floor laughing hysterically, just because one person let out a "hello" as Bruce walked past. Jessica found the laughter infectious and couldn't help laughing along with them, much to Bruce's annoyance, who didn't find it at all funny.

Jessica soon realised that, as a foreigner with blonde hair, she was getting a lot of attention from the locals. Many women would come up to her wanting to touch her hair and tell her how beautiful she was, asking Jessica for autographs and photos. At one point she was even approached by a smartly dressed Chinese businessman asking if she would like to be a model for his company, which she politely declined. She felt like she had been catapulted into another world, into another life, where she was a famous celebrity and everyone thought she was beautiful.

"China is an amazing place to be," Bruce enthused, telling Jessica about the opportunities available to foreigners. "Living in a foreign land, you can do anything you like, be anything you want to be, the possibilities are endless." Bruce admitted that he had fallen in love with the place, the people, and the culture. She caught herself thinking of Dr Wu and the commitment she had made to herself on that first night in China, to open herself up to learn and explore and discover China, along with her true purpose.

Chapter Thirteen

Later that night, as the two of them sat down for a local dim sum dinner, in a restaurant near her hotel, Bruce tucked into a bottle of rice wine, following an afternoon drinking beer and whiskey. Jessica had not wanted to drink and was finding the smell of alcoholic fumes on his breath quite overbearing. Despite years of infatuation for this man, Jessica was actually starting to feel uncomfortable with the closeness of Bruce's advances; a physical repulsion she certainly wasn't expecting to feel.

"Isn't it funny?" he slurred slightly, as he threw his arm around her chair and moved into her personal space. "I'm not your boss anymore," he said suggestively with a raised eyebrow. He had a lustful look she recognised, but it had never been directed towards her before. She recognised it was the look he used to give Anita the secretary, along with all the exchanges of giggles and flirtations.

With a sense of clarity, she realised the two of them had probably been having an affair all that time. *I wonder if that is why his wife left him?* she thought. *That explains why Anita had been so defensive every time I mentioned Bruce's name.*

"So…?" he said suggestively, moving his fingers along the back of the chair and onto her arm, walking them up towards her shoulders. "You can't tell me you haven't thought about it. Haven't wanted it. Now there's nothing to stop us…"

He leant in to kiss her, she could smell the rice wine on his breath. She pulled away feeling uncomfortable. She thought about Dr Wu and how different it had felt. How much she had wanted to kiss him.

There had been times when she may have thought about what it would have been like to be with Bruce. Thinking about his power and authority, protecting her and leading her to a better life. There had been times when she had felt pangs of all-consuming bitter jealousy towards Anita or Bruce's wife, as they got treated so well with spa vouchers by way of 'recognition', or perhaps it was guilt. Now she was the one with all the spa vouchers, with all the attention from Bruce and she realised that she didn't want it.

When it came to it, her body reacted on its own, her thoughts and emotions, which had been so scrambled in her head, became clear in that very moment.

"No, Bruce. Sorry no," she surprised herself with her assertiveness. "In fact, I am going off on my own for a few days, I need some time to myself." She heard the words coming out without realising that she had even planned to do that, or known that was how she felt.

"But Jess, I thought you had come to see me. I've

got used to you being around. I want you to stay here. I need you," he exclaimed, taken aback by her request to go solo.

"I know Bruce, I've had fun these last few days and I will come back and see you, I just need some time on my own. I've had a lot going on and I've got a lot to think about. I don't want to be dependent on anyone else, I want to find myself. There are things I want to do and I must do them on my own. I hope you understand."

He didn't speak as they finished off the meal, just knocking back glass after glass of very strong rice wine and getting redder in the face. She didn't like this side to him as she sat feeling awkward in the silence. She thought about all the drinking, the need for attention, the sulking and selfishness. She knew that he didn't really want her, he just didn't want to be alone. She had not known her own mind as strongly as she now did. She felt like she had broken through the haze of jet lag and worry, and woken up as a new person with clear determination. She quite enjoyed standing up for herself and what she wanted. She was physically and financially independent and now emotionally independent too. She was in charge of her own life and it felt empowering.

Did I ever really want Bruce in that way, or have I changed? she wondered, as she gathered her things. *I don't think that I knew what I wanted before, that was the trouble, but I am starting to get clearer in my mind and trust the way I feel.*

She now felt like a person in her own right, not just

a shadow of someone else, and she knew what she wanted. She longed to break free and explore her newfound confidence. She said goodnight and excused herself to pack up her belongings at the hotel.

* * *

The next morning, Sunny came to the hotel to say goodbye to Jessica. Bruce had apparently called her that evening after Jessica had left and demanded to see her, spending the rest of the evening pouring out his heart about how lonely he was, whilst continuing to pour out lots of rice wine. Sunny assured Jessica that she would look after him, confiding in Jessica that she actually cared for him very much. Jessica did not tell her about his advances and instead used the opportunity to gain some advice.

"Sunny, I want to go and explore China and I'm wondering where to go. I need some time to find myself and I want to discover more. Can you suggest somewhere?"

"Huangshan, the Yellow Mountain," she said immediately. "It's the most beautiful place in the world. They say that you need to climb to the top to find yourself, to find your heart's true destiny."

"That sounds perfect!" Jessica said, feeling excited and agreeing straight away.

Sunny made a few calls, booking hotels and trains for Jessica and writing it all down in a schedule. She handed Jessica some information and useful phrases, which she had kindly written in both English and Chinese, so that Jessica could point at the Chinese characters to get her there. They laughed together as Jessica tried to pronounce the various sounds and phrases, writing her own notes in the margins to remind her how they should sound. Unsure of what she was saying, Jessica kept going up at the end of each word and sentence, questioning if she was saying it right, which Sunny found hilarious.

"When your tone goes up at the end of a sentence, like asking a question in English, you change the entire meaning of the word," Sunny tried to explain through her laughter.

"In Mandarin there are four tones, and a neutral, so there can be five different ways of pronouncing the sound, which create different meanings of the word. This means that a word can mean several different things depending on how you say it. Tones can go up, down, down then up, they can be flat or neutral." Sunny tried to explain as simply as she could, but Jessica couldn't follow and just laughed. Sunny gave the example 'ma' which she explained could mean 'horse', 'hemp', 'mother', 'to scold', or to 'signify a question', like a question mark at the end of a sentence. Jessica's face showed how confused she was with the tones.

"Ok, ok, I'll teach you a very simple conversation," Sunny said. "To say 'hello' is 'ni hao', where 'ni' is 'you' and 'hao' is 'good'. So, hello is actually 'you good?' 'Ni hao' is pronounced like 'knee how', so think of asking someone the question how is your knee: 'knee how'?"

"Knee how?" Jessica practised as Sunny smiled and nodded as she continued.

"'How are you' is 'ni hao ma', so just as before, but simply also adding 'ma', which is like a question mark."

"Knee how ma?" Jessica carefully and phonetically asked.

"Good, good. 'Hao hao,'" Sunny laughed. "So, 'hao' means good. The word 'hen' is 'very', so if someone asks you 'ni hao ma', which is 'how are you?' you can say 'hen hao' which means 'very good'. Finally, you can say 'thank you', which is 'xie xie', which sounds a bit like a combination of 'sea-air sea-air' and 'share share'. To help you remember, think to 'share share' the thanks."

"Share share." Jessica thanked and practised the conversation starting with hello.

"'Ni hao.'"

"'Ni hao,'" replied Sunny, then asked, "'Ni hao ma?'"

"'Hen hao xie xie,'" Jessica beamed, delighted with her first Chinese conversational exchange.

After much laughter, and armed with the notes, they went to the station together and Sunny helped make all the arrangements and put Jessica on the train, even buying her Chinese style pot noodles for her dinner. They hugged and Jessica thanked Sunny for all her help and promised to see her again soon. Then she was gone and Jessica was alone at last.

Chapter Fourteen

Jessica felt an excited nervousness as she travelled to Huangshan, the Yellow Mountain. It was four and a half hours on the bullet train from Shanghai, and Sunny had arranged for a driver to pick her up and take her to the hotel at the base of the mountain that night. The hotel would allow Jessica to keep all her luggage there securely, whilst she climbed the mountain the next day.

Sunny had explained that Huangshan, the Yellow Mountain, was a very popular place as it was so beautiful, climbing it was considered an important milestone in someone's life. Sunny had said that whilst it was a good day's climb to the top, it had proper paths and steps, with stalls along the way selling water and snacks. She had told Jessica that there were temples built on the mountain and plenty of places to rest as she climbed, so it didn't seem too daunting.

Leaving the city, the landscape changed dramatically and the land opened up into fields. She saw buffalo and farmers planting rice, much more like the traditional image she had in her mind of China. The noise and pace of the city, which had blurred and saturated her senses, calmed to form a colourful picture of life in China.

It wasn't long before Jessica missed the comfort of having a translator and tour guide. She realised that she could not read, speak or understand the language. She was illiterate, and even when she tried to read the phrases from her tour book, she did not get the tones right and people just looked at her with blank faces.

Alone and unable to communicate with the world around her, by the time Jessica got to her hotel room she felt a bit homesick. She had an urge to connect with her life back home and people she knew. The hotel had a computer for guests to use so she started checking emails, but was unable to log on to Facebook, which was inaccessible in China. The comfort of being able to read in English, to connect and communicate with people again, was so uplifting after being immersed in a new language she couldn't understand. It was strange thinking about how everyone at home had just completed another week at work, whilst her life and the world she was now living in had changed so much.

She wrote a long email to Pam, apologising profusely for her behaviour and thanking her for everything she had done. She explained that she had relapsed into a moment of madness, and impulsively rushed off to China as a way of distracting herself and running away from her feelings for Dr Wu. She confided that she felt like she had found her soul mate in Dr Wu and cared for him deeply, but realised that she could not force herself onto him, that she had compromised his career by kissing him and that is why she wanted to run away. She told Pam that she had left Bruce in Shanghai and was now going to find herself on the Yellow Mountain. She hoped that Pam would understand and forgive her behaviour before she had left.

As she scrolled down, she saw that she had a new message. It was from Steve. She hovered, unsure whether to open it. They hadn't spoken in a long time and she remembered the meltdown she had after she saw his photos last time.

> Hi Jess, how are you? I hope this is still the right email for you. I heard about the company going under and letting everyone go. Sorry to hear about your job, but I actually think it's a really good thing for you, you worked way too hard. I hope that you're getting out there and having some fun, you deserve it. I know it's been a while since we've spoken, I'm sorry about the radio silence. I hope that you're ok and that there are no hard feelings? There certainly isn't from my side, in fact I would really like to thank you. You may not know it but you really helped me rediscover myself. I think I had become a bit of a 'try-hard' and spent all my time following you around like a sick puppy, trying to make you happy. I lost my own sense of self worth and purpose. When I came to Oz I was broken, I didn't know what to do with myself. But then I took some time out and focused on what I wanted, what I really wanted out of life and then I went for it. I've set up my own business here, I surf every day and have an amazing lifestyle, life is good. So, the big news, the main reason I'm writing, is that I've met someone and well, we're going to get married. Julie is lovely, the most amazing person, you would really like her. I wanted to let you know personally and not just have you see it on Facebook or something. I really hope that you are well and find happiness yourself too. All the best, Steve

Jessica read the email and was surprised at her reaction, or lack of it. There was no pain, no tears of emotion, no heartbreak. She felt relieved, even happy. She smiled as she sent a reply with bright bold colourful letters spelling out the word 'congratulations' and she genuinely meant it. She was pleased that Steve had found happiness and was living his dream life.

She felt relieved in a way that Steve was happy and that breaking up had been the right decision. She realised that they were never meant to be, they had not brought out the best in each other, or fulfilled each other. She had worked all the time, putting her work above him. He had never competed against her work, and if she let herself admit it, he had never competed with the infatuation she had with Bruce. Now, however, she realised that Bruce was not what she wanted either, he had purely been a distraction from herself.

Bruce was to her what she had been to Steve and the pedestals they were put upon were too high and unstable. Just as Steve had been with her, she had been living in Bruce's shadow for many years and now it was time to step out into the world as her true self. She realised that neither Steve nor Bruce could ever compete with how she had felt about Dr Wu and the connection she had felt through every fibre of her being to another person, physically, spiritually and emotionally; she had never felt that before. Even if she never saw him again, Dr Wu had woken her up to her life. She felt alive and truly grateful.

She realised that when Dr Wu had asked what her

heart had wanted she had known deep down, but she could not admit it to herself, she did not have the strength to bring it out into the open.

Removing herself from the comforts of her daily life, Jessica had stripped herself of everything and found in her heart the person she connected with on so many levels. But connected as she felt, as much as she longed to belong in those warm brown eyes, she felt ashamed that she had caused him embarrassment and discomfort when she had tried to kiss him. She knew that he had different cultural beliefs, and she respected that entirely. She loved him all the more for the honour and respect he showed to his family, how he put others before himself, even if it meant that his parents would likely be the ones to decide who he should marry. All she could do was to carry the thought of him with her, to continue on her own journey, taking all that he had taught her and continuing to learn. She liked the idea of helping others to grow and develop, as she had done with Dr Wu. Because of him she wanted to better herself, to be the best that she could be and that was a wonderful gift.

Chapter Fifteen

The next morning Jess woke up early, as the sun rose, filling her room with ambient light. She wasn't sure if it was the thin hotel curtains or the excitement she felt at being on her own about to embark on an adventure, but she woke up alert and fresh, aware of her heart beating, exhilarated at pursuing the journey she had begun. She sang to herself as she dressed in her black cotton exercise trousers, a vest top and cotton shirt over the top, wearing her comfortable walking shoes and packing a warm wind and waterproof jacket into her backpack. She didn't put on any make-up, or give any thought to how she looked, she didn't feel the need to dress to impress anyone. She was alive in the moment, finally accepting who she was, how she had got to be there, and what she was about to do. Nothing else mattered.

As she looked out the window at the rich red, pink and purple swirling sky, the sun rising strongly in the east, she was enthralled by the moment. The mountain peaks outside her window rose far up into the clouds.

"It's so beautiful," she said out loud, letting out a

deep breath. She was finally in the moment, not drenched in the past or fearful of the future. She was here, now, about to climb and conquer her mountain.

As she waited for the bus to arrive, she watched the sky changing colours and scribbled a little note in her book:

> Every day the sun rises and the sun sets,
> Filling the world with every colour of emotion,
> Reminding us time is precious and life is beautiful.

The shuttle bus arrived and Jessica got on, showing the ticket and permit for the mountain, which the hotel had provided for her. She read the information on the leaflet about the mountain:

> Huangshan is regarded as the loveliest mountain of China. The mountain range comprises many peaks, some more than one thousand metres high, often emerging from a sea of clouds. The magnificence of its scenery has been widely referenced in art, poetry and literature over many years.

Even though she thought she was early, life was in full swing all around her at the entrance gates. The air was thick with incense, as people bought large red incense sticks and prayed at the base of the mountain. Local men were loading heavy buckets full of all sorts of goods, placing the jam-packed buckets on either end of bamboo sticks, which they rested on their shoulders and set off up the mountain carrying their heavy loads. Locals had set up stalls, offering water and food, whilst others were selling tourist souvenirs.

She was even offered some rice wine by a man in a makeshift bar, who told her that it would give her 'strength for the mountain'. Declining the rice wine and going for a large bottle of water and some snacks instead, she felt prepared and ready to take on the mountain in front of her.

Looking up at the solid granite and pine covered peaks, stretching up into the sky, she took a deep breath of fresh air, before setting off up the endless steps in front of her.

Determined for the climb, Jessica put her head down, one foot in front of the other and set a good pace. The entrance to the mountain quickly faded away below the clouds. People selling drinks, food and fruit were scattered at intervals about every twenty minutes up the mountain. She would stop at resting points when she felt tired, then look at the local men carrying heavy buckets on their bamboo sticks and think, *If they can climb a mountain carrying all that weight, I can certainly do what I need to do with just me to support.*

A couple of hours into the climb, Jessica's legs were starting to ache from the narrow steep climb and she vowed to stop at the next resting point. As she approached a large flat area with stone seats around a shallow wall, she saw that a class of art students and their Master were lined up along the wall, painting the spectacular scene in front of them. She sat just behind them, watching five art students paint five different perspectives of the same mountain. One student had focused on a close up of one of the mountain peaks, whilst others had expanded the overall view to include several mountain peaks and blossom in the foreground. Many shades of browns and greens made the mountains come to life and pink and white blossoms brought detail and depth.

Jessica sat watching the creative construction of paint and brushstrokes, blending texture and styles, until each blank canvas became alive with the scenery of the mountain, telling its own story. Each was a true representation of the scene in front of them, but every perspective was so entirely different. It was interesting to see all the different styles and techniques, where each young student had their own idea of what the scene meant to them and the life they could bring to it.

It reminded Jessica of something she had read one night, when she had stayed in instead of going out drinking with the girls. The book had stated that we are each the artist of our life's work, creating our own unique masterpieces with the experiences we paint onto the canvas of our life. As she looked at the beautiful scene ahead of her and the colours of creation on canvas, she finally understood the meaning of being the creator of your own perception and therefore your own reality. She felt content that she was on the right track.

Jessica bought some fresh lychee fruits from a lady selling bunches of them from a makeshift table and sat trying to peel the exotic fruit, getting sticky fingers. Like grapes, they came on a stem, but each one had a hard and spiky outer shell, which once peeled revealed a soft white flesh, with a smooth untouched stone at the centre. Eating the delicious sweet juicy fruit in the sunshine, quenching her thirst, she thought it tasted a little like a combination of grape and elderflower. Jessica savoured the moment, the explosion of flavours and new textures, she felt grateful for the new experience. The sweet juicy fruit gave her energy for the climb ahead and she set off with renewed vigour.

As she climbed further she started to notice lots of metal padlocks on the gates and railings of the path. At first she wondered if people had locked something here once and left the lock behind, but as she climbed further the number of locks increased, until every available space was covered in them. She stopped to look at them and an older gentleman stopped beside her.

"Love," he said, with old smiling eyes.

"Excuse me?" she said, as she looked at the kind face of a wise old Chinese man, possibly in his eighties or older, dressed simply in blue baggy trousers and a long brown cotton shirt. She was full of admiration at the thought of him climbing all the way up there.

"Love," he repeated, motioning towards the locks on the gate.

"Ok?" she said dubiously, without having a clue what he meant. She wished that she could speak Chinese, instead of having to rely on everyone else to speak English. "Do you mean lock?" she asked slowly in her best clear English, smiling so as not to seem completely patronising.

"Lock," he said pointing to the locks and then

continued to repeat, "Love." He used his hands to demonstrate two lovers coming together and then locking their love to the railings.

"Ah, the locks are for love?" she asked, understanding his play of hands. "Lovers lock these padlocks onto the gates to show they are locked together in love?"

"Yes," he replied looking very pleased with himself. "Good luck for love. Love long and live long." He smiled, nodded and continued to climb the mountain.

"Love long and live long," she replied smiling back, thanking the kind man for the insight.

Jessica kept on going, climbing up and up, into and beyond the clouds.

If the men with the heavy loads can do it, and that kind old man can do it, then so can I, she told herself each time she started to tire. She was determined not to give up.

Further up the mountain she stopped to admire a tree covered in red ribbons, like a magical tree with red leaves dancing in the breeze.

A group of about eight Chinese students asked her for a photo. She assumed that they were asking her to take the photo of them, so she reached for the camera but they laughed and said they wanted a photo of her. Then each of them took it in turns to take photos, so that they could all get to have their photo taken with Jessica. As they did this they used it as an opportunity to practise their English.

"Where are you from?" asked one of the young men, smiling.

"I am from London in England," she said. "My name is Jessica."

"Ah, London. England." They repeated, seeming very pleased with this. "Nice to meet you, Jessica," a few people said at once.

"Lots of fog," one of the girls remarked, which baffled Jessica a little.

"Big Ham!" said one of the boys.

"Welcome to China," the other girl chimed in with a friendly smile.

"Do you like China? And Huangshan?" asked the first boy again.

Jessica didn't know who to speak to first as they were all talking at once, which was a little overwhelming, so she just picked the last question.

"Yes. I like China and Huangshan is beautiful," Jessica replied and all the girls giggled. They echoed her word 'beautiful', and one of them touched her hair. She wasn't sure what they were calling beautiful: China, the mountain, or her.

"Do you know Big Ham?" asked the boy again, eager to hear her response.

"No... err... no, I don't think so," replied Jessica, quizzically.

"England football. Bend it like Big-Ham," the boy said with pride and admiration.

"Ah Beckham, David Beckham?" Jessica laughed, realising what he meant.

"Yes. Do you know him?"

"No, I've not met him, sorry," Jessica admitted and the boy looked heartbroken.

"Can you tell me about this tree?" she asked.

"Why does it have all these red ribbons tied to it?"

"This is a special tree," answered one of the boys, who was a little more confident in his English than the others. "You write your wish, a prayer, or a special message on the ribbon and tie it to the tree."

"Really? That sounds fun. How do I…?"

"Here…" he said, leading her to a stall with red ribbons and pens. "You make a donation here and then write your name and a wish. Whatever your heart most desires."

"Thank you," said Jessica, pulling out her purse to make a donation, waving goodbye to the group as they headed up the mountain. She wrote her name and closed her eyes for her heart's desire. She thought back to the meditation and visualisation she had done with Dr Wu. How happy she had felt when she had finally realised that she was in control of her own thoughts and that she could transport her mind to go anywhere she desired. How Dr Wu had helped her to find herself, to connect to her heart, her life, and to live in the moment. There wasn't much room on the ribbon to write any detail so she just wrote two words big and bold: Dr Wu. She walked over to the tree and tied it to the first branch, wishing with all her heart that he was happy and would get this message of love she was sending across the world to him.

Jessica continued on her journey up the mountain steps and the number of people seemed to reduce as the path got narrower and steeper, until the point where it was almost vertical. The wide concrete steps lower down the mountain had now become small makeshift steps from rocks, which could only just about hold a foot if placed sideways. It then turned into a vertical climb with just footholds dug out into the mountain. Chains to hold onto were pinned into the rock, although they were so low down that it was almost more difficult to reach down to hold them, so Jessica resorted to practically crawling up the mountain on her hands and knees.

Jessica's legs were shaking from exhaustion and fear. She pushed herself to continue but she wasn't sure how long she could go on. She knew that she was nearly there, she was close to the top, she just needed to overcome her mind.

I'm not going to give up, she thought with determination, fighting her exhaustion. *I'm going to climb this mountain even if it kills me.*

She felt the air thin, along with the thinning number of people still climbing. The crowds early on in the journey had become just a few solitary climbers. It was late afternoon and the sun was losing its heat as she stood in the shadow of the mountain.

As she bent over, trying to catch her breath, through the dizzy stars in her vision, she saw a small path leading off to the side. She knew she was very close to the top, but needed a rest before heading up. It looked sunny and she felt like she could sit down out of the way for a minute or two for some peace and quiet.

She slowly squeezed between two weathered rocks and round the corner away from the main path. Her heart almost stopped and the breath caught in her throat as she looked in awe at the scene in front of her. She was filled with a sense of déjà vu. It was the vision from her dream. It was the place she had imagined repeatedly, lying in the holistic health and wellbeing centre in England, deep in meditation with Dr Wu.

The rock stretched about ten metres in front of her and there perched above it was a small arched tree with blossom gently falling like confetti at a wedding. She edged herself to the root of the tree and sat down beneath its canopy. She sat cross-legged and took a long deep breath of pure clean air; like water in a desert, it quenched her weariness. She felt like she was in a dream, in fact she was in her dream, the place she had dreamt about. *Am I actually here? Awake? Alive? Is this real?* she thought, feeling a calm sense of fuzzy contentment wash over her as the sun's warmth shone on her face.

She could hear nothing but the wind whirling past her and birds, free and wild, singing and flying and whooping in the currents of the breeze. Most of the birds she had seen in China, up until then, had been pets in cages. The old men took their pet birds to the park every day, where their cages would hang in the tree whilst the men played cards.

Here the birds are free, she thought. *Like me, I am free. I am here.* She smiled as she looked around her.

As far as her eyes could see was thick vegetation. It was like a bouncy green sponge, a mass of different shades and textures, sprawling over the sea of wave-like mountains rising from the clouds. The plants were covered with butterflies, mainly white ones, fluttering everywhere and birds chased each other across the path right in front of her. It was like a dream, her China dream, but this was now her reality.

She listened to the melody of nature all around her. She felt a deep connection to the moment, to the mountain, and the earth beneath her, realising her relativity and interconnection. It was like she was the girl she had seen in her vision. She closed her eyes, feeling the warmth of the sun filling her senses. She felt like she was filled with light, a pure energy flowed through her, connecting her to the universe and everything in it. She let go of herself, all her fears and conflicts, casting away her negative feelings of unworthiness. She was strong, she was alive, she was everything, and she realised that she had a lot to offer the world.

She had climbed the mountain and was about to reach the peak. She focused on what Dr Wu had taught her, on opening up her body and mind and listening to her heart. She took a deep breath in through her nose for a count of four, held it and then slowly released the air through her mouth for a count of eight. With each breath in, she focused on positive energy entering her and flowing through her, and her out breath was the release, taking away any feelings of tension and fear. She deeply breathed in and out like the gentle ebb and flow of the tides.

"Connect with the moment, connect with the breath," Dr Wu had taught her. Like a mantra, it was deeply embedded in her mind and his words echoed through her soul: "Be in the moment, be in the breath."

As she thought about his words, she thought about him. She felt full of love. Dr Wu was her inspiration, the key to unlocking her heart's desires. His words and example had changed her life and she aspired to be a better person, to help and teach others, the way he had with her.

Teach others… The idea danced in the front of her consciousness as she focused on this thought. *Teach…? Hmmm, but what could I teach? I don't have any wisdom or knowledge… No! I must be positive. Think about what I want and then focus on how to get it. 'What we conceive, we achieve'*, she remembered reading somewhere once. *I could teach English here in China. I know that lots of people in China are looking for native English speakers and I would love to learn more about this fascinating culture.*

She felt an urge to sing, to shout, to share her feelings of love with the world. She stood up and reached up into the sky, bringing her hands together as she had done with yoga and then releasing them out to the side, palms facing forwards, opening up her body like she was offering a hug to the mountain and life itself.

She felt impassioned, alive, inspired. "I can do anything in the world… and what I want to do is teach," she proudly announced out loud. She had not felt such certainty and clarity before and she liked the feeling it gave her. The power and strength of the mountain seemed to flow into her and through every inch of her being, rushing life through the branches of veins in her body. She was ready. She squeezed back through the rocks and turned the corner onto the main path, where she stopped still and froze mid-step.

Her thoughts instantly scrambled; her confidence and determination vanished into nothing but white light.

I'm hallucinating, she thought. *I can't tell the difference between reality and my dreams anymore. I've lost it!*

She stood paralysed, with one foot on the ground and the other half coming over a rock, with her knee bent ready for action. She felt like she was about to fall or to faint as she clung to the mountain for support.

Standing in front of her was Dr Wu.

The moment he saw her, his face lit up into a huge smile, his deep brown eyes shone so brightly they were dazzling.

"Jessica!" he enthused, as he bounded towards her.

"Err… What…? How…? What are you doing here…?" She managed to squeeze out, as he lunged towards her, knocking her from her precarious balancing act and catching her in an all-consuming hug. She steadied herself and got her balance back.

"Jessica, I am so glad I've found you," he said, as he squeezed her tightly.

"Is this really happening?" she asked. "I don't understand. Is this a dream?"

"Oh Jessica, this is real." He smiled kindly looking deeply into her eyes.

"But… what is… real… What is reality?" she searched, confused. "You once told me that reality is just the perception we create in our mind. Therefore, I must be dreaming. I know that you said that you could make my dreams come true but…"

"Yes, and you need to wake up to make your dreams come true," he said, with smiling eyes and then burst out laughing. "Oh Jessica, I have missed you so much." He embraced her again.

"You have?" She was so shocked and confused; she didn't know what to think anymore. "But, the kiss, I-I-I'm sorry," she managed to blurt out at last.

"No, I'm sorry Jessica, I didn't know what to do, I wasn't used to feeling that way. I didn't…"

"But, how did you find me?" she interrupted, trying to get her head around the situation. "How did you know I was here?"

"Aunty was worried about you. I didn't tell her anything, but I guess she must have sensed something was wrong with me and how sad I was when you didn't come back. Apparently she phoned your house and spoke to your housemate, Pam, is it?"

Jessica nodded, as they both sat down on the rock before she fell over.

"Pam said that she was worried about you. You had seemed very upset and she said you had gone to China. I wasn't sure what to think, but I was due a trip home to see my parents and, and… well I felt the need to come to China."

Jessica listened to the voice she had loved to hear, the voice that had guided her to this very moment. She reached out and touched his hand, to make sure it was real, that he was actually there. He opened his hand and took hers into his own, gently interlinking their fingers, rubbing his thumb over the soft skin on the back of her hand.

An Invitation . . . To the Life of Your Dreams

"I phoned your house and spoke to Pam yesterday from Hangzhou, where my parents live and where I have been staying. I felt bad. I wanted to check you were ok and to see if Pam had heard anymore. She said that you had been in touch and were climbing Huangshan today and so I came this morning. I knew that if I got to the top of this mountain I would find you."

"And, you did," she said, smiling.

"Well, not as easily as you might imagine," he said with a smile. "I got the cable car up and…"

"There's a cable car?" she exclaimed, feeling cheated after her struggle to climb.

"Yes, well I got to the top and couldn't find you. I spoke to a group of students who said that they met you by the prayer tree, they even showed me pictures they had taken with you, so I headed down the mountain to the tree. I didn't pass you on the way, and when I got there and you were not there I thought… well I wasn't sure. Maybe you had gone back down? Maybe it was a sign that I should leave you be… to be on your own and discover yourself."

"No, I…" Jessica tried to interject but Dr Wu continued.

"I went to make a wish and tie a ribbon to the tree and as I walked up to the tree, I saw it. A ribbon with your name on it, and then… my name. That was a sign all right. I charged back up the mountain and, well, here you are."

A silent tear rolled down Jessica's face. She didn't know what to say. She just looked into the deep brown eyes she knew so well without needing words. Dr Wu leant forward, wiped away the tear with gentle long fingers, and kissed her tenderly on the lips.

I love you, she thought with all her heart, and his heart responded back with a subtle dance, a fluttering rhythm and an overwhelming feeling of love.

"Dr Wu...?" she started to say.

"Ha, Jessica, please call me Lee," he said softly, as he pulled her closer to him with his arm around her shoulder.

"Ah, so your name is Lee?" she smiled.

"Yes, it's actually spelt Li in Chinese pinyin, but it sounds the same as how you say Lee in England, so I started spelling it like that in the UK to make it easier."

"Li Wu," Jessica practised out loud.

"Ha, that means a gift or present. My actual name is Wu Li, as we put the family name first in China."

"So what does Wu Li mean?" she asked.

"Well it is deeply poetic and like many Chinese terms, can be interpreted in different ways. It relates to the energy of the universe and can mean the enlightenment of the heart and mind. It's also like physics: the patterns of universal energy and matter."

"Wow," she said. "That's amazing and so deep and meaningful. My name is so boring in comparison."

"A name is just a title we give to something to help us place it in the physical world, to file it in the vast library we store in our mind. However, there are other things that we just seem to know, at a deeper spiritual level, we don't know how or why, we just know."

"Like intuition?" she asked.

"Yes, and there is a name we've given something in order to try to understand it. You knew me on a deeper level, before you ever even knew my first name. And I feel like I know you and have connected to you, even though at first I wasn't sure if that was allowed as your teacher. I tried to rationalise it, I even tried to ignore it, but I couldn't. I felt it deep inside, it's hard to explain."

"But what did you like about me?" Jessica questioned. "I was a mess."

"You are full of life and character, you come across as strong and tough, but you have a softer quality inside that is fragile and unique."

"Like a lychee," she said smiling; he smiled back but continued, not allowing her deflection of the compliment to stop him.

"You have a hidden depth within you, yet you fight it, trying to stop the world from seeing who you really are. When you first bounded into the centre, with your spirited enthusiasm and your desperate need to be liked and to fit in, it made me smile. But as we spent more time together, you relaxed and allowed yourself to be who you truly are. I saw the light in you, the love, the spirit. I felt your pain, I felt connected to you. I wanted to put a mirror up to you, to show you how I saw you, a beautiful woman who has been through so much, yet it has made you who you are. Instead of accepting who you are and being proud, you had been running away from yourself for years, blocking out your feelings, emotions, and what you truly wanted. Busying yourself with distractions. You have woken up to your reality now, to become your true potential. You have transformed into a butterfly. But like a butterfly, you cannot see the true beauty of your wings from your close-up perspective, it is only in standing back that they can be truly admired from afar."

Jessica didn't know what to say, she had never felt so valued, so understood by anyone, not even herself. She had heard that true love came from a deeper level, where you just knew and understood without needing words or reason, but she had never experienced it until that moment.

* * *

They walked to the summit together, it didn't seem far. Jessica didn't even remember the trek, it just felt like she was flying in heaven as she looked down at the floating clouds and out through the thousands of years of nature and beauty that surrounded them.

They sat on top of the mountain as the sun set and the sky changed through a palette of colours, then enveloped them in darkness. The stars shone brighter than she could have ever imagined. It was as if she was looking directly into the heart of the universe and seeing its mighty power and abundance.

They cuddled together to keep warm, under the thick jacket and blanket he had brought. Other people were also at the top of the mountain, they had set up camp fires and handed around hot sweet potatoes cooked on the fire, which they gratefully accepted, but they hardly noticed anyone else was there.

She told him all about her journey and he told her all about his. They talked for hours, yet time seemed to whiz by, as they laughed and cried and shared their stories, connecting on a deeply personal level. As the sun started to rise from the east and the sky turned to the most beautiful colours imaginable Dr Wu leant in and kissed her.

"Good morning," he said. "Welcome to a new day."

"But we've been awake the whole time," she whispered.

"Indeed," he replied knowingly, with a wide smile. "What time is it?" he asked.

"I don't know, it doesn't matter," Jessica beamed. "We are here. The time is now."

H. P. Carr left an award winning corporate career to go on a journey of self-discovery, researching alternative perspectives on fulfilment and happiness. Having lived and worked in China, she returned to write and volunteer in Asia during a sabbatical, before coming back to the UK to co-found a charity that inspires effective generosity. With a degree in Psychology and English Literature, she creates complex characters that delve deep into emotional experiences and to quote one reader 'provides a great psychological insight into human existence'.

Follow the adventure at
www.hpcarr.com